Heaven Will Find You

A story of hope, healing, and the afterlife

Sheldon Lawrence

STILLWATERS
P R E S S

Copyright © 2023 by Sheldon Lawrence

Previous Published as *Hearts of the Fathers*
by Sheldon Lawrence in 2016

All rights reserved. No part of this publication may be reproduced,
distributed, or transmitted in any form or by any means, including
photocopying, recording, or other electronic or mechanical
methods, without the prior written permission of the publisher,
except in the case of brief quotations embodied in critical reviews
and certain other noncommercial uses permitted by copyright law.

Visit www.sheldonlawrence.com

ISBN: 978-0-9977070-4-5

1

They have let me come and speak to you in your sleep. They said it would help us heal but that I should not go alone because seeing my son again in the flesh could pull me back down—my love could lapse into need or self-pity. So my friend, my guardian, has escorted me here and is watching me, taking care, ready to fill me with light if necessary. He is wise; even now, seeing you here, I long to be part of your life and wonder what might have been if I could have seen into your heart. But regret is heavy and can quickly drop into self-indulgent despair. I have come too far to risk that.

I want to tell you how I came to this point and where I have been since my death. I want to tell you about the hard path of repentance for someone with my stubborn heart and the difficulty of fixing things from where I am, close enough to touch you but separated by a universe. You carry so much of me within you— some good, some bad. I bear part of the burden you inherited from me, and I would labor for eternity if necessary to lift it from you. My greatest pain is knowing the burdens I passed on to you like a virus, and knowing that you will in some degree pass them to your children. I have learned how deeply our paths and eternal destinies are intertwined.

I used to believe we were all lone wolves dealing with our own problems, making our own way, succeeding or failing based on our own merits. But I was wrong. I have come to know we are not separate. We are parts of the same whole, a living organism. One of us is not saved without the other, and so on through the generations. When one rises, the entire organism flourishes; when one falls, the entire human family suffers.

We can make things right. That is the great truth, the beautiful mystery. You are still in the game, and I am one of legions cheering for you, encouraging you, and praying for you. You carry within you the hopes and burdens of your ancestors. Growth and repentance are so much easier where you are, in the flesh, but even here we are all involved in the work of salvation.

If you retain any of this, it will seem like a strange and disjointed dream. But I hope something I say will ring true to you. That one day while reading or in conversation, when you hear a truth, you will feel a resonance, like you have heard it before, that somehow it makes sense. I did nothing to teach you faith while on Earth, but now I can at least whisper this story into your soul and hope that it somehow finds a place there. More than anything, I hope that, even if only in your dreams, your heart can begin to turn toward me, your father.

*

The first thing I remember after the accident is the powerful urge to flee the scene. There, in the darkness of a remote mountain highway, lay a steaming mess of two mangled vehicles. I told myself I was going for help, but there was no question that I was running from the mess I had just caused, running from the consequences of my choices. I had been driving drunk and would be arrested when the police arrived. Moans of agony seeped from the other mangled car but I did not go to help. To my relief, and some shame, I survived the wreck without even a scratch.

In the distance I thought I saw a house and told myself I would go there and get help, spinning my motives to look more innocent than they were. Yes, I would run and get help. But my real reason for running hung in the air. I ran for the same reasons I had always run away, to escape, to hide from responsibility. I wanted the forest to bury me so its blanket of darkness would cover my sins. In the pale moonlight, bodies, now quiet, lay motionless in the twisted wreck, even a limp human form lay in my own car—one I assumed had been thrown into my vehicle on impact. My chest now sick and hollow, I turned to run.

I heard a distinct voice say, "Don't run." I looked to see who said it, but I stood alone in the cool night air. The voice came a second time, more like a warning, and seemed to come from within my being.

Above the highway a piercing light appeared, illuminating the entire scene. The light revealed not only the smashed cars, but the truth of the whole chain of events that hung in the air, an undeniable reality. The true cause of the crash, my intentions in running, the injured people in the other car—all displayed before me with perfect clarity.

I told myself the light was from another car, or

perhaps a result of hitting my head. But every time I lied to myself in the presence of this light, the absurdity of my thoughts were naked and obvious. If only in this moment I had submitted to the wisdom of this light, allowed it to open me and work its truth upon me, I could have been spared a lot of pain. The light invited me into it, but I resisted.

Now more than ever, I wanted to run. I could not bear the presence of the light and wanted to be as far from its influence as possible. The voice from within again begged me not to go into the forest, but I pushed it away and plunged off the embankment into the thick, dark trees below.

I slid fast at first, almost falling. What I thought was a small embankment leading to the flat bottom of the canyon now plunged deep into the darkness. I did not drop into a canyon, but an abyss, a dark pit that would hide me from the all-knowing light at my back. As I pushed downward through the darkness, the voice of warning grew fainter with each step, and then finally, to my relief, fell silent.

I finally reached the bottom of the canyon as the ground gave way to a gentler but still downward slope. I could no longer see the steep wall I had stumbled down. Nothing about the landscape looked familiar. I was now impossibly far away from the wreck, worlds away, it seemed.

The moonlight was gone, replaced by a soft gray mist. A bone-chilling emptiness pervaded the atmosphere. I kept walking, not knowing what else to do, still lying to myself by saying I was looking for help. In the dim light I saw a grove of trees ahead, a tangled mass of branches and undergrowth. I hesitated.

A voice, somehow familiar, came from deep within the forest. "Look! It can still see you. The grove will protect you. Hide!"

I looked up in the direction of the wreck and could still see a pinpoint of light like a single star in a black sky. The voice was right. The light still watched me. Though distant, my movements and thoughts were as obvious to it as when I was directly under its gaze. Seized with the fear of being captured (by what or whom I could not tell) I ran into the grove, pushing deep within until the spark of light above was no longer visible.

Beyond the trees—or was it deeper in the forest?—human voices laughed and whispered.

"Hey!" I shouted into the darkness. The power of my own voice—loud and forceful—startled me. Anger and frustration welled up and my voice felt violent. The buzz of alcohol no longer blunted my senses. I felt more alert and alive than ever.

I pushed on toward the direction of the voices, but the forest grew thicker and darker. I was no longer among living trees but only thick, finger-like shadows, sometimes snagging me and holding me back, not like branches so much as hands. I ripped off the clinging branches. Laughter echoed in the trees, faint at first, but then louder.

"Shhh…not yet, not yet. Let him get deeper."

Was it a real voice or just inside my head? I couldn't tell.

"Who's there?" I yelled.

Again, the aggressiveness of my own voice

frightened me. My anger did not have a particular cause, did not rise from a specific wrong against me. Rather, the resonance of the atmosphere seeped into my being. Rage clouded the air like smoke, and I breathed it in. A beast grew inside me, nourished by the waves of violence and hate that filled the grove. As my anger surged, so did my physical strength. I clenched my fists and teeth. I could fight, or kill, anything. I dared something to challenge me. The lie of looking for help no longer motivated me. I pushed through the trees because they were in my way, and I wanted something to fight against.

Every thought irritated me. The accident, though now like a distant memory, infuriated me. If it weren't for the stupidity of the other driver, I wouldn't be wandering through this forest looking for…whatever I was looking for. I didn't care if those in the other car survived. Their death would be their problem. Something softer inside me listened in horror as I said aloud, "I hope they're all dead."

The few voices in the forest—or in my mind— now became the indistinct murmur of a crowd. Sometimes laughter, sometimes a cry of pain, sometimes frustration, and sometimes all of these at once. I went mad with confusion. No way could so many people be here, in the middle of nowhere, at the bottom of a canyon. But they watched me, counted my every step, studied my every thought. The trees watched me, the shadows watched me, and then they followed me. Behind me, the path collapsed and closed in. Ahead, black veins sprouted from the ground to slow my steps.

The branches now grabbed at my face, my feet. Did I wonder how shadows and trees could have intention? No, I only took pleasure in hating them. I snapped them away with strength I had never before experienced. I was an animal, busting my way through the undergrowth. When a tree wrapped a limb around my neck or my waist, I ripped it away with ease.

A joyless laughter came from deep in the shadows, a mocking, triumphant laughter. I stopped and listened in the darkness.

"Show your face," I yelled. "Bring it on!"

Only a faint, suppressed laughter, then nothing.

The sudden stillness reminded me that I had no clue where I was or where I was going. The car wreck felt like a thousand miles away. Should I turn and fight my way back up the hill? I couldn't detect a trace of the path behind me, but only a grayish light illuminating an ocean of tangled shadows. No more canyon walls, no more light in the distance.

One moment, fear coaxed me to turn back, the next moment, rage prodded me deeper into the forest. Voices crowded my mind, mostly my own, complaining about the person who crashed into me (their fault, no doubt), my job that made me take that trip, and this pointless trek into the woods.

I pushed on through the tangled mess of trees, but they no longer felt like trees. Rough bark was now smooth and cold, like—I didn't want to admit it—the skin of something dead. The shadowy branches now bent and coiled like snakes. One reached down and caressed my cheek and neck, pulling away when I reached for it. Another jabbed me hard in the ribs, and

I grabbed it and pulled it apart, its flesh tearing in my hands. It shrieked in pain, but the cry was only a mocking one followed by laughter, like when a child proves it isn't really hurt.

This should have terrified me, but I converted terror to anger. The oppressive atmosphere overshadowed any sense of good judgment or even self-preservation. As if in a dream, I did not stop to wonder at the moment, but simply took the world as it presented itself.

My most overwhelming desire, the most obvious thing to do, was to fight someone. My rage transformed me. Nothing was stronger than me. I now dared them to come for me, these voices, whatever they were.

"He's almost ripe," said one of them. Shadows melted into the shape of human forms. Like ravenous dogs waiting for their master to unchain them, they howled and lunged.

"When?" they cried. "When?"

There were now hundreds of them, perhaps thousands. I turned to run, but tendrils wrapped my body, binding my legs and arms, forcing me to the ground. Like a fly caught in a web, the more I struggled, the more I sent waves of excitement through the legion of beings creeping toward me. They planned a long time for this, and now came to reap their harvest.

Finally, an authoritative voice from the darkness let them have their reward.

"Now."

2

My son, I will not disturb your dreams with the horrors I endured that night. I will not burden you with my nightmare, but you should know something about what I suffered there.

I would later learn I was what they call a fresh kill. As a new arrival from my mortal life, I still carried the pain of living within me. My fresh sadness, frustration, and disappointments fed their appetites for some glimpse of their old lives. They savored these emotional energies like a sweet delicacy. I fought like a lion, but in fact they were the lion and I was a mouse, mauled and abused for their entertainment.

Every time I cried out or fought back in the struggle, they howled with ecstasy. The attack did not relent until my will to fight collapsed. They abused and tortured me in every way imaginable. Their cruelty, their appetite for violence, knew no limits. It was a feeding frenzy, and I was their prey.

Whenever my will to fight weakened, they backed off until I regained strength and rekindled my anger, and then they would maul me once again, prodding me to fight back. They howled with delight with every reaction they won from me.

I fought for what seemed like an eternity as they swarmed me, taking turns inflicting and enjoying pain. When I finally gave up, they grew bored and, at the order of someone with authority, left me to wallow alone in the total emptiness of that realm.

For that was how I now perceived it, a realm, a dimension. No forest trees surrounded me, no starry night or chirping crickets. Earth, with all its comfort and familiarity, disappeared into nothing. Had the impact of the wreck caused a hallucination? Would I awaken in a hospital bed, relieved from a feverish nightmare? No. I had never felt more alive. Never more alive, but never wishing so much for death, for the total extinction of my soul.

My attackers left, releasing me from their grip. But in their absence, something worse settled in: an awareness of being lost in an abyss of nothingness. I entertained no hope of escape. This was my eternity, to exist as nothing in a bottomless pit of nothing.

In life, no matter how bad things got, there was something to hold on to, some bit of hope to get me through another day. But here I sunk into a vast and infinite nothing. No kindness, no help, no beauty or mercy, just emptiness layered upon emptiness. I could not stand. I could not move or speak. I was not asleep. I was not awake. I had no sense of being in a particular place in relation to another place. I had no sense of now or later or forever.

That is why, when I heard him speak, it felt like a

kind of rescue. Though his voice sounded like death, it saved me from a universe of nothing.

"Pathetic," he said. "You didn't give us the fight we deserved." He was the leader who commanded the attack. He came into view. The dark silhouette of a being stood over me.

"This isn't real," I said. "This is only a nightmare."

"That's right," he said. "You're in a nightmare within a nightmare. And you will never wake up."

He went on, speaking in cryptic aphorisms.

"You are not alive and you are not dead. Life and death are one. All is death without dying. All is life without living."

Though his presence emanated hopelessness and dread, I wanted him to keep speaking. I wanted contact with another being, however hideous. I preferred to bind myself to someone in fear than spend eternity alone in the darkness.

When he perceived a subtle shift in loyalty toward him, when he sensed my craving for contact, he began to teach me.

"I am your master," he said, not as a proposition, but a factual statement.

In life I was a willful, stubborn soul, and I resisted the thought of cowing to anyone.

Sensing this resistance, he abandoned me in the darkness, and the horror of complete isolation set in again.

When he came again—whether a hundred years or a few moments had passed, it felt the same—and said, "You will call me master," I easily complied. Anything to keep him near.

And so his teaching continued. When I accepted him without question, when I submitted myself to his authority, he rewarded me with more contact.

He did not want me to analyze his teachings. If I asked questions, he would isolate me until I begged for more of his knowledge. My place was to obey, not to ask, and not even to comprehend. Whenever I felt like I grasped some idea, he would contradict it with something exactly opposite. The slightest questioning, the slightest hesitation in accepting the inconsistency, would result in new punishment.

"There is no God," he said. And I would fully accept this as a fact. He then said, "God wants to destroy our freedom."

"But if there's no God, then how…"

He disappeared, retreating into the shadows, leaving me in timeless isolation. If I could have counted minutes or hours, sunrises or sunsets, I could have endured the loneliness. But I had nothing to cling to, no rope that dangled into this pit of eternal nothing.

After seeming eons he reappeared and said "You're even stupider than I thought, and I've been watching you for a while. Let's see if you understand: God wants to destroy our freedom."

I repeated the phrase.

"I don't just want words. Believe it," he commanded.

I repeated until I fully accepted its truth.

"God and freedom do not exist," he said. He waited until I believed, and then continued.

"The only pleasure that matters is commanding

another being and watching them obey. Even now, you believe that you have choices, free will," he chuckled at the words. "But I hold you in my hands. I can do anything I want with you. I am your god now." The black outline of his body leaned in closer. "I command, you obey. Unquestioning obedience is the first law of hell."

I recoiled.

"You resist. That's good. It makes this even more fun for me. You want freedom? Look where your freedom brought you. You want choice and free will? I've watched you for a long time and your choices are worthless. Everything you choose turns to failure," he laughed. Now I felt he spoke the truth, something I could easily accept. A lifetime of bad choices washed over me.

"What about you?" I said. "You're here too." I braced for punishment, for isolation or violence.

"Yes, I'm here too," he said. His soft reply made me sorry for challenging him. "I came to continue the work I started in life. I was once a priest, a grand inquisitor, charged with re-educating heretics like you, idiots who believed in a rational universe where one could make rational choices. But their choices didn't bring them to freedom. Their choices got them tied to my stake, where the burning cleansed them of their delusions."

He smiled, and I could see his face now. I had expected to see the image of a devil or a demon. But the more he came into view, I saw the form of a man, a human who had once lived on Earth and like me had indulged in his darkest impulses. A human, but stripped of any shred of compassion or empathy. Not even a glimmer of light shown in his pale eyes.

"If you were a priest, then you believed in God," I said.

At this he laughed long and loud. "You believed that little story?" In a moment, laughter stopped and his earlier rage returned. "Stupid, gullible man. You don't need to know who I used to be. Right now, I am your god. That is all you need to know. Say it."

I repeated it until he was satisfied. Then he said, "Everything I have taught you is a lie."

His teachings came like nonsensical riddles I was forbidden to unravel or contemplate.

"The foundation has no foundation. Nothing can be known, for there is nothing to know."

Then, at the end of every lesson, he would say, "All I have told you is a lie. Repeat it until you believe it." And when I had fully accepted that, he would say, "All I have taught you is the only truth you need." Nothing in the teaching resembled coherence, reason, or sanity. There was nothing to grasp onto, no concept, no idea that didn't fall apart the very moment I tried to hold it in my mind.

Confusion and contradiction echoed in my mind. If there was a theme to his teachings, it was that absolutely nothing was real, nothing was true. Even the idea that nothing was true was not true. He destroyed all hope of building upon a foundation, of somehow pulling myself back into sanity. His jumbled teachings occupied my whole mind so that the mental noise, the grappling with problems with no solutions, drowned out memories of life on Earth. My thoughts formed a hopelessly tangled maze with no beginning and no end.

Any form of self-reflection brought instant retribution, a barrage of insults or isolation or both. The one question I was never to contemplate was, *Who am I?* The answer was absolute and unquestionable. I was nothing. I did not exist. I had no separate reality. I was a dream within a dream, a vapor in the darkness. I was a whimper that would soon fall silent. When I tried to remember my life on Earth, to grasp onto some identity, he flooded me with so many confusing and paradoxical claims that my mind grew incapable of reflection. I became a cauldron of confusion, anxiety, and resentment.

When my education was complete, he introduced me to his followers, who also called him master. I learned that he also had a master, a hierarchy that extended down into even darker realms.

He was master of the hunt, the tenuous leader of one of the countless gangs in this region that stalked and captured fresh human souls. His dominance in the gang depended on his ability to deliver on the hunts. But his dominance did not inspire loyalty or affection. We hated him and he hated us. We only begrudgingly accepted his leadership for his experience and skill in hunting wandering souls.

If we wandered or disobeyed him, he threatened to strike us down with lightning. This threat at first seemed absurd, until I occasionally saw powerful flashes of light in the distance, making shadowy spirits scatter like mice. The rumor was that when a soul was struck, it just disappeared. For all we knew, it had been annihilated, never to hunt again.

The master told me that if I would submit to him completely, he would teach me to hunt.

"Hunting will feed you the life you crave and liberate the souls enslaved by the Tyrant," he said. Earth was a prison, a world of slaves. When we hunted a soul we liberated it into the freedom of our world, where, outside the surveillance of God, it could pursue any pleasure it wished.

As soon as I accepted that story, he furiously denied the existence of the Tyrant, the Earth, the universe, and life itself.

But I didn't care about the reasons for hunting. I now longed to hunt, to make another soul suffer as I had suffered and bask in the waves of pain. My body, or the dense field of energy that was now my body, became ravenous with desire. I hungered to feel something, anything, and in this place, only pain satiated my hunger.

During my life on Earth, I had nurtured my anger, this animal within, believing that it was my greatest asset for getting ahead in the world. I was demanding, uncompromising, seizing the weaknesses of others, always advancing myself and tearing down everyone who got in my path. I measured people by their ability to advance my own agenda. This was not visible to the average person. Friends praised me as a hardworking, ambitious man. But no one knew the rot spreading within me.

In mortal life healing influences kept the sickness at bay. I never realized how much I benefited from the residual light of others and how little I contributed to that light myself. I lived like a parasite, sucking life from others, not realizing my own decency came only in response to the goodness of others. A stranger holding a door open for me, a smile from the overworked lady at the checkout stand, a good laugh with a friend—these infused me with enough light to keep living. But rarely did I initiate these moments of grace. They came to me, not from me.

Now, in the absence of light from others, nothing could slow my downward spiral. The energy in this realm amplified, but did not create, the darkness I flirted with during mortality.

My condition was not unfair or unjust. God did not create this hell as a punishment for bad souls. No higher power sent me there. This was simply a place where like-minded spirits gravitated to their own kind. Among us dwelt souls from every century and every class and every culture—warriors, merchants, prostitutes, preachers, and politicians. We came from the ranks of respectable citizens as well as the dregs of society. We all sank to the same level of resonance, free to become exactly what we desired. We ate the fruit we had cultivated so diligently during life, a bitter harvest sewn in a million choices.

Just as great as the mystery of God's love is the mystery of God's commitment to freedom. Like His love, His freedom is absolute. God's nature loves and allows. Our immature human love clings and controls. For many spirits, freedom is the only thing more terrifying than Hell, and so they choose Hell instead of the awful responsibility of choice.

So it was never God's authority I resented, but God's freedom. I wanted God to just tell me what to do. But the question always came back to me: what do *you* want? What do *you* desire? Unable or unwilling to answer that terrible question, I let the world tell me what to want, which was wealth, power, and the gratification of every appetite. If God would not just tell me what to do in order to earn his approval, I would get the approval of the world. At least I could tell what it wanted from me.

Perhaps I accepted the authority of the master hunter so easily because the world had conditioned me to seek approval. The more he hated me, the more I wanted his approval. And the more I wanted his approval, the more I hated him for it.

This seemed to be the pattern throughout Hell—a deep mutual hatred, a need to control and blame and abuse one another, coupled with an abiding need for each other. Although we insisted on our own independence and freedom, nowhere in the universe can you find such needy and dependent creatures as the souls in Hell. It would have been impossible for us to simply walk away and leave one another alone. There were no gates or chains keeping us there. But we needed one another to play the roles of victim, abuser, manipulator, and liar, in a never-ending drama. I never heard new ideas, new arguments, new insights, only the same petty backbiting playing out again and again.

Hunting new arrivals was the only thing that offered a small amount of variety to our existence. A fresh kill from the mortal world fed us new pain and provided a new recruit who could eventually join our gang, once we crushed their will entirely.

But hunting required a level of skill and

concentration uncommon in dark plain, and therefore needed special training. At the end of my initial teaching, the master told me that if I wished to hunt with him, I must obey him without question, and that it was his right to abuse and discipline me as he saw fit. I would be an underling in the background and could only get the leftovers. Someday, if I passed "the test," I would move up in rank.

When I asked about the test, the master said, with a sense of sick pleasure, "It's time you met someone, the one who led us to you. Your rescue from the Tyrant was his test, and he passed it easily."

A man was brought forward from the masses of dark forms.

"We do not choose souls randomly," said the master. "We just finish the job you started in life with people you know."

The man's face and form took shape. I recognized him immediately, feeling his presence more than seeing his person. I had become one of his kind. I had grown to hate him in life, and now, in death, my contempt reached full fruition. Before me stood my father.

3

We did not delight in seeing one another—no surprise, no embrace, no desire to remember past times. No affection could form between us in this realm. That we ended up in the same place made perfect sense. When he died, we hadn't spoken in years, and I took satisfaction in skipping his funeral, judging him for what I believed was a cowardly choice to leave the world.

"A family reunion!" laughed the master. "No tears for the old man? Father and son don't want to play ball?" Sneering laughter echoed from the gang.

I detected in my father a hint of remorse, a desire to talk to me alone. But rather than softening me, the idea only enraged me. The master, nervous at my father's softening heart, led him away from me. I lunged at him and tried to land a blow. My father wanted this, wanted me to hurt him to have at least some contact. The master smiled at my aggression but didn't allow me to touch him. He sent him away to hunt in another pack, and I took my place at the master's side.

In my life I blamed my father for everything wrong with me, every addiction, every break up, every career failure, and now that blame magnified in my mind. Nurturing my victimhood, I harbored fantasies of hunting him down and making him pay for his crimes against me, offenses which, in this environment, took on grotesque and exaggerated proportions. But soon after our separation, the memory of my mortal life faded into a fragmented dream.

I felt no desire to talk with him or explore what had become of us. Such reflection was hardly possible now; my mind couldn't sustain one line of thought for very long, let alone explore mutual understanding. Our brief meeting was the last I saw of him. I heard later that other gangs rejected him and that he wandered alone until he challenged a master hunter, who blasted him into oblivion with a bolt of lightning.

This news did not surprise me, as it was consistent with my broken memories. He always made his own needs and problems the center of everything. I didn't care much where he went, and never gave him another thought.

Why didn't I stop to consider what was happening to me? Why didn't I reflect on how one moment I was fleeing a car accident and the next I was roaming with demons? These horrors had become my normal life and I could not imagine or remember any other possibility. Perhaps the only thing worse than living in Hell is growing accustomed to it, believing it to be the only reality. Once drawn into an insane world, one also becomes insane.

The most frightening thing was that I couldn't tell if the mayhem of this world lived inside or outside my own mind. I couldn't distinguish between my thoughts and the thoughts of others. Though we insisted on our intelligence, our importance, our power—above all, our individualism—we were dreadfully the same. Confusion flowed from one mind to another in a monotony of self-importance and self-indulgence.

To live inside my mind with my own compulsive negative thinking was hard enough in life, but to share in the collective mind of other sick souls was to be lost in a sea of fear, confusion, anger, regret, and despair, with nothing to grasp on to. I had no ability to sustain a rational thought for more than a few seconds.

The noise coming from the self-tormented souls was relentless, from howls of laughter to groans of agony. We fought, we gossiped, and we perpetrated upon one another every abuse and perversion imaginable. But fulfillment never accompanied indulgence. Hell echoed with cries of desire that never found satisfaction.

But the hunt held promise for something genuinely new and exciting. I absorbed the master's lessons.

"How far are we from your old life, your so-called friends and family?" asked the master. The question confused me. Distance meant nothing here. I had fallen into a different universe.

He answered his own question with an air of indifference, like he was bored at having to teach me. "There is no far or near, only up and down," he said.

"We cannot go up, so we must pull down."

This did little to clear things up, and he grew impatient. "They are right here," he said. "Look closely. Feel them." This was the first time I had ever been encouraged to feel or concentrate, and I hardly knew how. I quieted my mind, and vapors of dim light appeared and disappeared before me. The light was only a wisp at times, but sometimes took the form of a human body.

"The soul is layered. We can work with the darker layers that want to dance in our kingdom."

He explained that fantasies of vengeance, jealousy, addictions, and over-indulgence in bodily appetites dropped the frequency of spirits into a spectrum that became discernible to us. In this state, we could not only share in their pain, but feed it as well.

At first he only allowed me to observe this work. The subtle process required great patience and flawless timing. We could not actually see the physical layer of the beings we hunted; our dimension vibrated at a far lower frequency than Earth's. But when a living human soul drank in darkness, it resonated with us and took shape, moving among us as a ghostly light. Most living souls never came within our reach, at least not for very long. But when they did, we could add fuel to whatever evil they entertained.

"You see this one," said the master, pointing to a dark red, ghostly image that appeared to be walking. "Look at the hate here, and the shades of envy here and here. Someone's having a terrible day," he laughed. "Now come, feed it so that it will feed you."

I focused on the being, directing hatred toward it.

"Your hate does nothing. Who cares if you hate it? Taunt it. Provoke it. Tell it how worthless it is."

With his guidance I harassed the poor soul until gradually it took shape. Loathing filled its body until I saw a full human outline. The angrier it grew, the more pleasure I took in the work. As it responded to me, ever so subtly, I felt powerful. I breathed in its energy which infused me with something resembling human life.

I pushed harder, wanting more. Then the soul vanished, and the game was over.

"Idiot. You moved too fast," said the master. "Too much too soon can scare them away. You have to make them believe these thoughts come from their own minds."

"What happened to it?"

"It doesn't matter. It'll come back. We've been watching it for years."

My training continued in this way until my skills were honed. We roved the land looking for new prey, new forms dipping into our dimension. We told the spirits of the futility of their lives and whispered stories of their victimhood. We exaggerated any hint of self-defeating, self-destructive thoughts they entertained.

On the earthly plane their bodies went about the regular business of mortal life, but we were like sharks, circling beneath, nipping and grasping the aspects of their soul that dangled before us. The smallest thing could lift a soul beyond our reach—laughter, joy, or unexpected kindness from a stranger. But the more we coaxed them downward, the more they took form in our dimension and became ripe for harvest when they left their physical body.

My first potential harvest ended in disappointment. A soul we had cultivated for some time neared its physical death, and we waited in great anticipation. Its body had been shot in a fight—one we did not create but had encouraged. The body took its last breaths, and once it released its soul, it became a visible and distinct form before us. We could see it, and it could see us. An overzealous demon flung itself upon the soul, snarling and howling, which obviously frightened it, causing it to cry out to the Tyrant in desperation. In an instant it was consumed in burning light that scattered us in every direction.

I only felt the disappointment of losing the prey. If I had been capable of thinking about this event a little more, I might have wondered where the soul had gone and why.

Most physical deaths ended in similar ways. But occasionally we had some success. If a tormented soul ignored the beckoning light, we could carefully reel him in. If we could keep a new arrival in a state of fear, or anger, or frustration, if we could set the hook before he realized he was dead, then our chances of success improved. If we could trap him in self-importance, self-loathing, or self-anything, then we could draw him in slowly. When whatever residual light in his spirit had dimmed enough to allow us in, we attacked.

I can't say how much time I spent on these hunts. It felt like ages, but there was no correlation to Earth time. Now, remembering that period, I can hardly use the word "I" to describe the creature that had overtaken my true self. Deep within me was still a spark of divine light, but it was so buried beneath my appetites and my deranged psyche that it no longer guided me. I had become a hardened shell, a grotesque body constructed from the energy of that realm.

Any sort of repentance requires stillness and self-reflection. Distraction kept us restless and agitated, except for during the hunt. Hunting proved dangerous to the monotony because it provided the only time for stillness. We had to quiet our minds as much as possible so as to not scare away the prey. The master warned us that he would punish any thoughts not focused on harassing our victim.

I had once seen a punishing strike from a distance. A man in another gang had become still and reflective and unresponsive to his master's commands. In an instant he was struck with a bolt of energy that consumed him. "Destroyed for stupidity," said the master. The flash was terrible, blinding, even from a distance, and sent dark spirits fleeing in every direction. The flash of light exposed us to one another, and for even that fraction of a second, the sight was hideous. It was not uncommon to see distant flashes throughout the vast plains of Hell. Only rarely did they come close enough to cause harm. But the mere thought of being destroyed sent fear throughout the enslaved souls and kept them in submission.

One of the only true things the master warned about was the power of the lightning. He was right to warn us. But he only pretended he wielded this awesome power.

He had good reason to fear it. I thought I was the

hunter, but in fact someone hunted me. Someone watched my every thought, every movement. A hunter far more skilled than my master stalked me with great patience. And he was preparing to make his move.

4

The master called me to his side, where he sat elevated from the group like some self-styled king. I came to understand the absurdity of this so-called master. In fact he resembled countless spirits in this place—petty, cruel, insecure. I hesitated to approach him. Would he punish me, banish me from the group?

"You will lead the next hunt," he said. "You are the best one to capture this soul. You'll just finish what you started in your old life, dragging him down, showing him his place. You know this soul's weaknesses and vulnerabilities. You know its capacity for self-hatred because you fanned those flames throughout your life. You laid the foundation. This prize belongs to you. It is your harvest."

This was my test, my full initiation. If I faltered, if I hesitated, I would be struck down. The master warned that he would punish any second thoughts.

"In life this soul embarrassed and disappointed you. Now you have the chance to get justice, to give the punishment its mother protected him from. You sacrificed everything for this soul, but it appreciated nothing and gave you nothing back. Now it's your turn. Now you can teach it the consequences of rejecting you, of pushing you away. It will learn to respect you now."

The master repeated the story until I no longer questioned it. He strengthened me for the hunt.

I was to lead the hunt against you, my son, because I knew your weakness better than they. I knew your insecurities. I knew your memories. I did not think of these memories as shared moments. By this time I was so far detached from my life in mortality that I only thought of them as tools to work with.

The master emphasized again and again how privileged I was to have this opportunity and that his own masters watched our progress closely. And for the first time I sensed in him something like fear. Someone higher—or lower—in Hell than he had charged him with this task. His status also depended on the success of my hunt.

Now, remembering this, I can hardly comprehend that my reality had become so twisted, so distorted, that pleasing this devilish soul mattered more to me than protecting you, my own son. Though we hadn't spoken for many years, I would not have considered inflicting pain on you like this. And yet, in a sense, I had. As the master reminded me many times, I had hurt you in life, knowingly and intentionally. This hunt only continued that work.

When the time came, we found you easily. Because of my connection to you, I led the way each hunt. Travel never involved covering distance. It was a matter of resonating thoughts. And because my thoughts, for good or ill, had been so connected to you in mortality, the master used me as the compass, the guide for the group.

Most of our successes were small. You were barely discernible, and many times we could not find a trace of darkness to latch onto. I did not know what made you so happy and hopeful at this time in your life, but your soul bathed in energies far above us. We circled like sharks below, but you flew in clouds well beyond our dark waters. Now I know you were in love, that you had been dating a beautiful woman with whom you had much in common. During this time of joy you disappeared entirely. Sometimes small, shadowy fragments of your soul appeared, but nothing to work with.

But our patience paid off. On one occasion, we found you in complete despair, and your form began resonating visibly in our realm. We only had to fan the flames of whatever darkness had overcome you.

Your thoughts grew solid enough to take the shape of language.

"I can hear him," I said. No one else could hear the words.

"Listen carefully," said the master. "If you can hear words, it will make our work easier."

The master, encouraged by the darkness in which you swam, openly hoped that you would take your own life early. He worked himself into a frenzy and lost his patience.

"Focus," he commanded. "Don't let him go."

I had not had a moment of peace or clear thinking

since I entered this tormented world, and now he asked me to still my mind and focus specifically on something outside myself. In his enthusiasm for your destruction, he made this fatal mistake. He didn't realize that someone more skilled than any of us also listened carefully, waiting for the right moment to strike.

My mind calmed and I heard your thoughts, your inner voice. But your voice alone didn't stop me. In your voice I heard a thought that had once been my own. It was a thought that, during my mortal life, filled me with both hope and terror. Your thoughts repeated themselves again and again. Fear and self-defeat spilled from your soul. But also, beneath the thoughts, something like hope, though faint and distant.

I am not ready to be a father, you said. I can't do it, you said. Again and again. Then you said you could not do to a child what I had done to you. The child itself, with all the responsibility, did not make you afraid. You knew the source of your own self-hatred and did not want to pass it along to this unborn soul.

In your girlfriend's womb grew your first child, and you wanted to run.

"He's afraid," said the master. "Feed it, feed it! He's not up to it. He's not ready. Complicate it. There's no way out. Hopeless, hopeless! It's his life or the child's!"

But in the stillness of mind, in my focused and single-minded state, something else, something other than the thought of your destruction, slipped quietly into my broken soul.

I no longer thought of you as my prey but

remembered you as my son. I knew you, and I knew your thoughts. Yes, I had known we hunted you, and that we were somehow connected, but I couldn't fully ponder what I was doing to you. But now, in the quiet, a faint and distant memory of myself as a human being came into my awareness.

A tiny ember of light within my chest began to glow, and, for the first time in what seemed like an eternity, I felt hope for you, that somehow things could be different for you and that my hell did not have to become your hell. My master looked at me in horror and tried to distract me, but it was too late. The other spirits could see what was happening and ran away in terror. They knew my punishment was coming, and so did I. Yet I did not care; I wanted to stay a little longer in this tiny spark of hope, and would endure annihilation to drink another sip of faint light.

I had, in my quiet and weakened state, let go of the resistance, the protective shield I had carefully built in Hell. I was now naked, vulnerable.

My master hissed and snarled and screamed the worst abuses imaginable. I braced myself for his attack. Energy began to gather and swirl high above me. But instead of commanding it, he backed away in fear. The lightning was not his. He knew it. And he knew more capable hunters were about to make their move. They had been waiting for the right time, patiently watching me, looking for an opening.

When I looked up to see the source, it struck with devastating power.

5

A shaft of pure white light shot down into the top of my head and surged through my body. The light came like an arrow from some distant region. To an onlooker it might have appeared as lightning, a bolt of electricity. An explosion of energy surged through my spine and limbs, back up my spine, into my brain to tear open my eyes. The dense shell that had become my demonic body shattered and burned in the glowing energy.

This was no crude weapon, but an arrow of light fashioned with a care and intelligence unknown in our realm. The hunters who shot it knew their prey, and they expected success. The lightning was not just energy, but intelligence. It came poison-tipped with a memory that penetrated my being upon impact.

I call it a memory, but it was more, not a mere projection of the past, but the living reality of a specific moment in my life. I was there, even more there, even more present, than when I first experienced it.

I stood in a delivery room in the maternity ward of a hospital. I knew every detail. Outside, the chill of autumn hung in the air. Fallen leaves splashed yellow and red on black pavement.

Your mother lay in the delivery room, young and sweaty and tired and beautiful. She had labored for hours, and now the doctor consulted with us. The baby's heartbeat, your heartbeat, was dropping, indicating stress. I could feel the tension, the sense of urgency in the doctor's words, though he maintained a professional demeanor.

He recommended an immediate C-section. I could feel how hard your mother took that news, as she had so badly wanted to have our first child naturally. I felt her heart, how it ached for your arrival. I felt the doctor's heart, urgent, pounding, ready to start the surgery. I saw myself, powerless, frustrated. Then I sensed you, your life, how your spirit stood at the doorway between worlds, how it desperately wanted to be born. You knew it was time to leave the comfort of your mother's womb, and you wanted life.

I could hardly watch them prepare her for surgery. Her body shivered on the cold and sterile operating table, as they poked and prodded and cleaned. They strapped her onto the surgical bed, arms stretched out and pinned down like a crucifix. One of them poked her belly with an instrument.

"Can you feel that?" he asked.

"Yes," she said. She shouldn't have felt it. The men talked. Maybe it had been too long since the last epidural, they said.

"She's already had quite a bit; it's already been a

long night," said one.

"But we can't proceed like this, not if she can feel it."

A man with glasses thought for a moment and made a decision.

"Spinal block," he said.

They unstrapped her arms and helped her sit up. Her whole body trembled from the cold and the medicines that coursed through her veins. She couldn't support herself, so the men held her. My young self wanted to hold her but could not, for I was not clean, not sterile. I had to be separate, behind the curtain that separated us like a veil.

The man with the glasses drove the needle into her back and probed with it. He was looking for something; the right place, it had to be the right place, but he couldn't find it. He pulled it out, found a different sized needle, and pushed it through the flesh of her back in a different spot. His eyes sweated. He couldn't find it. He pulled it out, and a mixture of clear fluid and blood streamed down her back. Red-faced, embarrassed, he made another decision.

"Let's try another epidural," he said.

Her body still shook from the effects of the last. The monitors beeped the sounds of two lives. The heartbeat of one of the lives, the smallest one, your life, had slowed steadily. The doctor knew it. The man with glasses knew it, and I knew it.

I pointed to the monitor and yelled, "Do something!"

Now, as I watched the scene as a spirit, I could see my anger expand like a wave through the room and mix with the others' fear and frustration. I could feel their bodies tighten and their thoughts thicken like mud. I made the moment about me, so that now the doctors had to think of me instead of only your mother and your unborn self.

The second epidural worked, and they laid her back down. She shook violently.

"I can't control my head," she said with blue lips. "Hold my head down against the bed."

Unknown milligrams of drugs coursed through her body. Her head trembled and her arms involuntarily tugged at the straps.

The procedure began. New machines started up. A vacuum sucked bloody fluid through a tube and deposited it in a jar. I held her head down. It was the only thing I could do, so I tried to do it well. I made it firm but comfortable. I caressed her pale, swollen face, which, in spite of everything, still had a small smile on it.

I watched your heartbeat on the monitors, and with each passing minute it slowed to what they were calling critical levels. I watched your mother's oxygen levels drop as well. I sat by her head, touching her, stroking her hair, telling her that I was there, that everything would be all right. Such empty phrases.

The epidural moved too far into her upper body, numbing her chest and lungs. She thrashed and gasped for breath.

"I can't breathe."

"You can breathe," they said. "You just can't *feel* it because you're numb." But she continued to gasp. Her oxygen still dropped.

"She can't breathe," I screamed. "You're going to kill her."

"Get him out of here," said the doctor, and I was escorted from the room, sobbing and cursing. In the hallway I did something I had never done before, not since I was a child. I prayed. I begged that, if there were a God, that He would save my wife and child. I swore an oath—an oath I would soon forget—that I would change my life, that if they were spared, I would seek out this God. I repeated the prayer again and again, like a mantra. An undeniable comfort descended on me. At the time, I assumed this resulted from psychological self-soothing. But watching the scene now, as a spirit, I saw a glowing field of light cover me like a blanket.

In time, a gurgling baby's cry came from the room. A nurse emerged and said that both the mother and child were doing fine. It started a little rough, but everything was just fine now.

The scene shifted, and I saw and felt myself holding you in a state of wonder. Labels like "baby" or "son" meant nothing. What I held in my arms was mystery and beauty. I could feel again the softness of your skin, your smell, the hospital blankets. I sat beside your mother, who smiled weakly at our creation. When I looked into your tiny, squinting eyes, still adjusting to the harsh light of this new world, I knew I would never be the same, that our destinies were forever connected.

The shaft of light embedded this memory into my mind, or rather, awakened it from within. That scene was one of the few moments of purity in my life. In that instant I loved you without complication, without expectation, without need. I loved you for no reason. You hadn't done anything; you hadn't earned anything.

As the hospital scene closed, I found myself again in darkness, except for a small thread of light extending upward from the top of my head into the infinite void. When I looked up, the thread of light brightened and began to swirl. White light transformed into ribbons of color penetrating the inky atmosphere. The thread turned into a rope, and the rope opened into a tube. The vortex roared like a tornado. The tunnel itself sang harmonious chords, but the vibration clashed with the dull, disordered vibration of Hell. The tunnel split the darkness, pushing it back, but looked as if it could collapse at any moment.

The hollow shaft of light extended not only upward but down into regions below, places even darker than the one I was in. Beneath me I saw hands reach into the tunnel only to recoil in pain. Above me the tunnel contracted into a fine point of light. The light beckoned me, inviting me in.

But the light also laid me open. I could not deny the truth of who I had become and where I had been. Reliving the hospital scene was the first time that I had been human in this cold world. It was the first time I had a complete recollection of who I was. It was also the first time I made a connection between the baby in my arms in the hospital and the being whose fears we had encouraged and fed upon. Consciousness of this truth wracked my soul. From the depths of this abyss, I had baited and taunted my own son. I understood with perfect clarity my failure as a father and my lifelong journey into this nightmare world.

Was this my punishment? Had God sent this light to mock and expose me, to rub my failures in my face?

"Go away!" I screamed into the light. I longed for darkness again. I longed for the thick clouds of Hell to swallow me up into its oblivion. Better to sleep through a bad dream than awaken into that awful reality that stripped away every lie I had lived by.

At these thoughts, as if the entire universe were a genie granting me my heart's wish, the tunnel began to weaken and fade. I realized I had, in part, created this tunnel and that I could strengthen or weaken it with my own intentions.

Below me, the tunnel began to collapse, and I could see the darkness closing in. Then a voice from above, a calm and familiar and penetrating voice, said firmly, "Look up and ask."

There was no question what I was to ask for. I must ask for help. Part of me, the part that was still in Hell, revolted at the thought of asking this exposing light for help. I wanted it gone, and I didn't need help from anyone. I was doing just fine. A thousand voices in my broken mind protested the light. Who did this voice think it was, offering to help me, as if I were some weakling, a nobody? Didn't it see I was a free man? I didn't take orders from anyone.

But part of my soul still basked in the beauty of my one-time family, the softness and vulnerability of your body, and the purity of your tiny spirit. My soul yearned for that reality, longed to live for eternity in that moment in the hospital. Only remembering my unworthiness and failures thrust my consciousness back down, so that the all-seeing light would leave me alone forever.

The tunnel below me continued to collapse and had now reached my legs. I felt the gravity of the darkness enfolding me, pulling me downward. The master hunter returned to my view and I met his eyes, which now held a look of satisfaction as I returned. I would be his once again.

The voice from the light above called out again, but more distant.

"The time is now," it said. But the noise that reentered my mind washed it away. I sank in the darkness, like quicksand, until it reached my chest. The tunnel above me could no longer hold it back. Gray, sickly hands reached into the tunnel, clawing, grasping.

A thread of light was still working its way into my chest, but I had been resisting it. Then, for a brief moment, I let in the light once again. I let down all my defenses. For one last time, I wanted to hold you in the hospital before slipping back into the place I belonged.

The light came in and this time taught me. It told me that the moment at the hospital was not in the past. It existed as it happened forever and ever. It possessed a separate reality, and any perceived failures that came after could not destroy it. In that moment, I was a good father. I loved and cared for my family. The moment lived forever, pure and undefiled.

If that moment contained indestructible goodness, then perhaps something good in me could also live forever. Maybe within me burned a spark of love that darkness could never extinguish—a part of me that God would not let wander lost forever.

When I caught hold of this thought, everything that was left of me wanted to believe it. But already the voices of Hell returned, shouting seductive lies and easy-to-believe insults. My mind was too weak to hold on to the good thoughts, and I felt them slipping away. I could not sustain them alone; they slipped from my grasp as the tunnel faded into wisps of light.

Before the voices of Hell completely repossessed my mind, I looked up and reached into the fading light and I cried out the only words I had left, perhaps the last words anyone can cry before again slipping into insanity.

"Help me."

No sooner had the words left my body than another bolt of lightning came from above. But this time the light took the form of a hand reaching down to catch me.

6

The grip was firm, but gentle and loving. I felt the energy of this being pour through my arm and into my body, healing and lifting every part of me. It had been so long since I had made contact with another soul in a way that was not violent. Just to touch his hand was to regain strength and sanity.

The tunnel opened again, this time into a strong, straight shaft of light, and again I heard loud, rushing wind as the tube descended into the darkness. The being who grasped my hand was beautiful. Strength and wisdom emanated from his person, and I knew that nothing, no power in Hell, could lay a finger on him. In his presence, I was safe. He was my guardian.

Light poured from his body into my own, drawing me along. It wasn't so much that he lifted me as that I flew with him, upward through the tunnel at the speed of light, as if we were light itself. The tunnel pierced the layers of darkness, and as we rose upward, the darkness dissipated like a lifting fog. Suffocating weight lifted from my chest—a suffocation that I hadn't been aware of. I could breathe now, free from the crushing density of Hell.

The tunnel dissolved, but we still traveled through space toward a brilliant light. The light was alive, whether with one life or infinite lives, I could not tell, but it pulsated with love and creativity and pure, indestructible joy. It was not just beauty, but the source of beauty. It was not just love, but the source of love. To part of me, it felt like home, like the most natural and necessary thing for me to do would be to join this light. But another part of me remembered who I was. I looked away from the light and into my body, and I could still see darkness within it. I remembered my mortal life and the pit I had dropped into once I died.

No creature from Hell could belong to the place my guardian was taking me. I would burn in the presence of that love, that light. I would be destroyed, and if I weren't destroyed, I would wish I had been. I could not bear the thought of my own darkness polluting that place.

"Stop," I cried. "I cannot go."

To my surprise, my guardian instantly respected my wish and stopped.

"I can take you to be healed," he said. "No one comes already pure."

This was the first time I had heard my guardian's voice. It was full of wisdom and love. He knew everything about me. I noticed now that he was not alone but attended by others. I wondered who they were, and instantly the reply came that they were my council; they were my friends and would help me for as long as it took.

These were the most radiant beings I had ever seen. It had never occurred to me that a living thing could be so beautiful. They had been human once—I somehow knew this—but to call them human would do violence to the reality of their present state. Somehow I knew intuitively that some of them were my ancestors. One of them, a woman by my guardian's side, was not related to me, but had some purpose to fulfill with me that I was not allowed to see.

But my affections were particularly drawn to my guardian, whose hands I still grasped and never wanted to let go. I was his chief concern, the focus of his mission. He had been tracking my every move in Hell, waiting for the right moment to strike. I could not make out the details of his face, as halos of golden light surrounded his form.

Was this God? Was this the Christ I had heard about and dismissed during my mortal life? At this thought, a kind of joyful mirth came from my rescuers. "No," said the woman at his side, as if I had spoken my thoughts aloud. "But he is, for the moment, a representative of Christ to you."

I doubted I could be worthy of such a guardian as the one who held me, and I wondered why some lesser soul had not been assigned my case. This was no ordinary being. In him were stillness and wisdom and deep familiarity with everything I had ever done, everything I had ever been. In life I always found a way to spin my motives, to tell partial truths or exaggerations. I played the game of making things appear a certain way. The reality of a situation didn't matter as much as how it came across.

But none of that was necessary or even possible with the being who now held me. If he was not God or a high angel, then he must have been some kind of spiritual master or prophet from ages past.

"We'll help you clean up, my friend," he said. He said it so casually, as if I had just fallen into some mud and needed to freshen up before dinner.

But I knew I could not bear it.

"I can't be cleaned," I said. "I am filth itself. Wash away the dirt and there would be nothing left of me."

The light in the distance—Heaven, I assumed— was not for me; I could not imagine myself belonging there. I cherish the thought that it existed, that the universe had some such reality to it, where others better than me could go. But that I had any part in it was impossible.

"It's not only possible," said my guardian, perceiving my thoughts. "You will not rest, you will have no peace, until you find your way back. You can take the long way if you choose, but eventually Heaven will find you. Everything you do, whether you realize it or not, is part of your journey back to Heaven. No soul is lost forever."

But I would not hear him. He didn't know who he was dealing with. Even being in their presence felt like an imposition, like I had forced them to descend into the sewer to pull me out, a wriggling and grimy thing, naked and ashamed.

I had to protect them from me and the trouble I would cause them.

"Please let me go," I said. "Find someone more worthy to work on." I pushed myself away from him, from all of them, and turned. The relief was instant. Though not a shred of judgment came from them, in their presence I could not help but judge myself. I wanted only to be alone, to hide. My choice hurt my friends, but this would be the last pain I would cause them and they could go back to the light while I went…where? I hadn't really considered what would become of me. I wanted to leave their presence, even though I didn't have a plan. I only wanted to fall.

The memory of Hell returned and filled me with horror. I looked below and saw layers descending into ever-darker planes. I was not falling by the force of gravity; my desire to escape the truth-telling light pulled me downward to a place I could find comfort.

But not Hell, I prayed. *Anywhere but there again.*

I was suspended in between worlds. Horrified by Hell, but also unwilling to submit to that pure light that would wash me into oblivion.

Then a thought came into my mind as if from somewhere else, somewhere outside myself. *What do you desire?* This was the great and awful question that the universe, that God, asked and always stood ready to answer. *What do you desire?*

At that moment, it was clear what I desired. I wanted something familiar. I wanted what I had known, what I had been used to and comfortable with. When this desire took hold in my heart, my descent slowed as I passed into a tunnel of a grayish light and then finally stopped when my body reached a kind of equilibrium and found resonance with its surroundings. The tunnel disappeared as my new environment came into view. I was home.

7

After spending a seeming eternity in the dull, dark monotony of Hell's featureless plains, the sight of even just one familiar object would have seemed like Heaven itself. But now the world I knew so well opened before me. I saw city streets, damp from recent rain, smelled the bacon and french fries from a main street burger cafe. Beautifully ordinary people carried stuffed bags from boutique clothing shops. In the distance, clouds draped mountain peaks. Everything rushed my senses with detail and clarity I had never before experienced. Was I in some lesser heaven, some place better suited for a guy like me? No, I was back on Earth. This was indeed my heart's desire, and my wish was granted, a prisoner released into freedom.

I could have spent an eternity soaking in the scene before me. In life I would have labeled it a boring, medium-sized American town, but to me it was beauty itself. A man held a door open for a stranger following him into a hardware store. A mother wiped a blob of ice cream that had fallen onto her daughter's lap and showed her to lean over the ground in case more dripped. Even the trees lining the city street struck as a remarkable human achievement. Someone, at some point, took thought to design their place in town, then plant and care for them. I perceived not just the trees but the line of intentions that brought them into being. How could I have never seen this before? How could I have taken all this for granted?

I looked below me and saw a maple leaf that had fallen to the sidewalk. The longer I looked at it, the more it revealed its secrets. Still green, not an autumn leaf, but splashes of yellow speckled its jagged toothy edges. Beneath this, a textured network of veins had distributed nutrients unevenly to the leaf, weakening it. Embedded within it was the information of all that had happened to it and around it. The insects that munched it, the rain that had fallen upon it. It was its own book of life, and the story it told was just as important and interesting as any story I have heard. The leaf had meaning and purpose. It was not a means to an end. It was complete in itself.

Everything I looked upon had a history, a life. Everything was worthy of contemplation. As I looked up into the tree from where the leaf had fallen, I must have desired to be there, for in a blink I found myself there, hovering in the treetops, watching them sway gently in the breeze. As a spirit, desire was motion. My heart pulled me to whatever it wished for.

I looked down at a little girl walking her dog and then found myself next to her. I looked at the top of a nearby church spire and found myself there, perched high above the city, taking in the scene. I flew around the town at the speed of thought and could control my speed by how much I contemplated the things that came within my vision.

This lightness and freedom were pure ecstasy to my soul. In Hell, movement had been like pushing through thick oil. Now I was an eagle freed from years of captivity. Even mortality could not compare with this freedom. Unburdened by flesh and blood, I soared as high and far as my thoughts could take me.

I experimented with this new power, thinking of familiar places. All I had to do was picture a location in my mind, and there I was, observing the scene. I tried foreign cities—the Eiffel tower and Paris at night, the Opera House at Sydney, and the top of the Golden Gate Bridge. I could drop into cars on the freeway and observe the passengers, sometimes seeing their thoughts and desires.

This was my childhood fantasy, unlimited access to all the world, and, best of all, I was invisible to Earth's inhabitants. I was free, and not a living soul could see me.

I thought of visiting you, my son, but instantly put it out of my mind. The horrible memory of having stalked you as prey was still with me, though it seemed like a distant nightmare. I swore I would never disturb you again. I also knew I couldn't bear to see you and the burdens you carry, knowing so many of them were my own.

I considered visiting the scene of my death, the place of the car wreck, but that thought sickened me. That place had been my gateway to Hell, and I wanted to stay as far away as possible. I was not ready to learn the fate of the passengers in the other car, and I knew the scene would tell me the truth. The trees, the rocks, and the road—they could not lie.

I didn't really want to visit my mother, same as in life, but the pull of my childhood home was irresistible. I felt a need to drop in and see the old place, not out of nostalgia, but perhaps to confirm the reality of my earthly existence. Disoriented from my journey through dimensions and unhinged from regular time, I needed to locate my past somewhere in space, as if to confirm that my life on Earth was not just a dream.

With only a thought and desire, I was standing in my childhood home. Outside I saw my aging and widowed mother "scratching in the yard," as she used to say, getting flower beds ready for spring planting, though spring was still weeks away.

I thought this would be a simple matter of looking around and remembering some old times, like seeing a photograph. But unlike the other places I had visited, my spirit-body tuned into the surroundings, as if the walls and furniture and trees suddenly noticed me. Embedded in each object was the story of its past, and much of that past included me. I found myself swimming in a bewildering sea of old energies, both joyful and painful.

My mother leaned the rake against the house and came inside, placing her gardening gloves neatly on a shelf. Her body had aged more than I remembered. I say her body because I perceived her spirit as youthful and full of hope.

I had always assumed she never remarried out of loyalty to my father. She often made comments to this effect and even put on a sad and resigned face when talking about her widowhood. But the woman I saw now was joyful and free. She loved her independence, but I could tell she felt some shame for loving it so much. She was happy to be rid of him.

I realized I had never known her. I had only known her as a character in my life story. What I saw now was not a character, not a role. She was not, to my surprise, a *mother*. Motherhood was a role she had played on the stage of life, but she could have played some other role just as easily.

She poured herself a cup of coffee and sat down with a newspaper. The house and its objects began to speak to me. I say speak, but it was as if my spirit read them, scanned them for information. Memories of my childhood washed over me in waves. I had come to the house to find steady ground, but now I was swimming in my past, and I didn't like it.

Yet strangely I felt a pull to remain there, to explore the place, to relive the past and to make sense of it. Or maybe I longed to return to my childhood self and be cared for in my home once again, to remain a ghost and walk the halls. It was a dark and lonely feeling, yet somehow seductive, like it was the only place I belonged.

Feeling drawn in like this scared me, and I willed myself to leave the place and never return. I vowed then not to visit any family members, including your mother, from my old life, wanting to avoid the hard memories they would bring.

So I spent months wandering. Though I did not belong to Earth time, I could still mark it by observing the passage of days, weeks, and seasons. I dropped in on old friends, snooped around my work, watched movies for free, as I thought of it, and spied on every forbidden and secret place I could imagine, simply because I could.

I suppose I must have been what people call a ghost, but that is not the right label. I was a solid and substantial being. There was nothing vague or wispy about my person. The Earth, on the other hand, appeared to me as a kind of hologram. I could pass through walls and doors, not because I was insubstantial, but because they were. From my frame of reference, I was real, and everything else was ghostly.

And it was this fact that began to weigh on my soul. What began as fun turned into crippling, excruciating boredom. I was alive but not living. True life is to live in relation to other beings and other objects, but in my state, I only observed them without relationship. Though they seemed within reach, right before me, they were hopelessly separate. Living mortals were protected by a faint shell of light. When I got too close to someone, the light pushed me away. The people and objects I observed might as well have been on the other side of the universe.

Being unable to interact with an environment that I loved so much was unsettling. Nothing could respond to me. So much of life in a mortal body is the pleasure of real people, even solid objects, responding to or resisting or somehow acknowledging your existence, but now everything and everyone ignored me. It was all out of reach. I longed for any kind of sensory experience, absolutely anything.

My craving for sensation and responsiveness became ravenous. I longed to taste a hamburger. My heart ached to contribute to an interesting conversation. I tried to get into arguments with people who could not hear or see me. Casual pleasures in life now became obsessions.

Appetites can be taught patience when there is at least hope of their satisfaction, but as the world paraded constantly before my eyes without a chance of gratification, my appetites became fierce and driven. Unable to find satisfaction, they grew exponentially. I would have done anything for a drink of wine, a taste of chocolate, a kind touch from a gentle hand. I wanted to hug someone, to hit someone, anything to interrupt the tediousness of observing but never participating. I was trapped in a movie, unable to interact with the characters or contribute to the plot.

When I thought I was about to go mad, a woman appeared as if from nowhere. She was beautiful and somehow familiar. I would have mistaken her for a mortal, as she wore plain blue jeans and a white blouse, but she looked directly at me. And although her being emanated a kind of light, she did not have, as the mortals had, a protective cocoon of light surrounding her person. She seemed unusually happy to see me.

"It looks like you've gotten a little lost," she said. "Would you like some help?" I was not used to being part of peoples' conversations now, and at first it was hard to comprehend that she was addressing me. This was the first time someone had spoken to me since my return to Earth.

"You're like me!" I shouted. I felt myself come alive again; finally someone was able to see me, respond to me.

"Yes, I have become more like you while down here," she said. "Have you had enough of this world yet?" It struck me as a rude question, but there wasn't the slightest ill intent behind it.

"No," I said. "That's the problem. I haven't had *any* of it. Do you know something I don't know about how to touch and feel? I was sent back to Earth, but it isn't working. It's no good. Everything is just a ghost of what it was."

"Didn't you get your fill during your mortal life here?" she asked again.

I didn't have time for this. I had hoped she could help me, teach me what had gone wrong.

"No," I said. "My life was cut short. Now I've been sent here for a second chance, and it's even worse. I wanted to go home, but this is some kind of trick."

"We didn't send you anywhere," she said.

We? It was impossible that this woman was part of my rescue. In the presence of my angels, I felt only reverence and awe. I would never have treated them like regular people, like equals. This woman was nothing like the beings who rescued me from Hell.

The truth, I would learn, was the exact opposite. Of those assigned to me, she was among the strongest, the most resilient, and the least likely to become entangled in the lower energies of Earth. It now pains me to know what a sacrifice it was to dim herself enough to descend into the cave of that world.

"You chose to come here," she continued. "You insisted on it, in fact. But are you sure this is home? Is this really what you desire?"

There was the question again, the terrible question about what I wanted.

"What I want," I said with obvious irritation, "is to live again, not just drift from place to place."

I paused and doubted my resolve. I must have also wanted an argument. "Is that what I should desire? You act like you know something I don't, so just tell me what I should want."

"You can't be told what to desire. You either desire something or you don't. Your heart doesn't lie; it can't put on a show to impress. But I can tell you this; you must carefully consider what you desire, for God stands ready to grant your heart's wish and let you experience the consequences, good or bad."

She meant only kindness, but I viewed her words as patronizing and condescending.

"You're here to preach to me? Did you rescue me from Hell just to toy with me and keep me in the dark?"

"Nobody's doing anything to you," she said. "That's the great secret. You are no one's victim. You're just all tangled up, and we want to help set you free. The universe offers places a lot more fun than this."

"I'm having plenty of fun. That place you were leading me to, I'm glad it's your thing, but it's not for me. Neither is getting lectured about my choices."

Before leaving she said what, in hindsight, I should have taken as both a hopeful promise and a warning.

"When the student is ready, the teacher will appear." She walked off then and disappeared in a flash of light.

I was surprised at how annoyed I felt in the presence of this beautiful being. My appetites and cravings had become my obsession, and anything that did not help me in my goal to re-engage life became a great irritation.

For days I flitted about, cursing my predicament until eventually sinking into depression. Flying around the world and exploring hidden places held no interest. Human life bored me so long as I could not participate in it. I fell deeper into despair. I sensed myself physically sinking, becoming heavier, denser, more earthbound. I lost the ability to fly, or was it I had only lost the desire to fly? I did not fully understand that ability and desire were the same thing in this existence.

As I spiraled deeper, my surroundings took on a grayish hue, and movement felt thicker and slower. But new beings, new people came into view. Before, I had seen only living mortals, but now a new group of souls became visible. A layer of light surrounded mortals, but now the landscape was populated with these denser beings who emanated no light.

Now that I could see them, they could see me. I must have looked lost, for I soon attracted their attention.

A friendly looking, easy-going man approached me. He wore cut off jeans and a cabana shirt opened at the chest. His jet black hair was pulled into a ponytail.

"Hey man! Welcome to the party," he said. "What's your pleasure?"

8

He was, since my death, the first regular-looking person I had seen, and this must be what made me trust him so quickly. I wanted desperately to be his friend, and I'm sure he sensed my neediness. I told him briefly what had happened to me since my death, and he became very interested.

"Sounds like you almost got snatched up by the Shiners," he said, referring to my angelic rescuers. "Good thing they didn't suck you all the way into their organization. They probably mean well with all their God-talk, and maybe someday I'll go and see where they hang out, but they don't seem to have much fun. Trust me buddy, the real party's here on Earth."

"That's what I thought at first, but I've been bored out of my mind."

"That's because you've been doing it wrong."

I knew there must have been some secret, some trick. I was filled with new hope.

He introduced me to his friends, and they took me in immediately. I finally belonged. This was familiar; this was comfortable. Maybe that prudish lady had taught me something after all. I followed my desires and now finally felt at home. I wanted a teacher, and he came into my life when I needed him.

They called him Raven, and he was the leader of the group, but no dictator like the so-called "master" in Hell. He was laid back; to him, no problem was worth worrying about.

"Show me what to do; show me how to live here," I said.

"It's all about the ride," Raven said. "The ride is everything; it's why we're here and what keeps the party going."

"The ride?"

"You already know you can't touch this world," he said. "At least not like when we lived on it for real, not now that we're ghosts. Isn't that nuts? Ever think you'd be a ghost going around invisible, spying on folks? But that's the thing, man, you gotta embrace your ghostliness. You see all these morons trying to grab somebody's whisky or smoke their weed. They don't get it. That stuff's gone for good."

"But here's the deal, with a little practice and patience you can get yourself a contact high." I leaned in and hung on every word. He knew he had me. "You see, we can't touch their bodies, but we can feel their spirits or souls or whatever you want to call 'em. Their spirits are still hooked into their bodies, so if we can feel their spirits, we can feel their bodies too. So when you're all synced up with them, you get off on whatever they're gettin off on, see what I mean? They get wasted, you get wasted with them. They go to some strip club, you're right there with'em!"

I shrunk back. This sounded too familiar, feeding on the lives of the living. I cringed at the memory of my life in hell, stocking and provoking hate in unsuspecting souls.

"Oh it's nothing like that!" said Raven, perceiving my thoughts. "Man, you've seen some nasty stuff since you died. The big man upstairs threw you right in the slammer! No, we don't attack nobody around here. We just get real close to them, you know, hook into them so we can party with 'em. See what I mean? Contact high, like from the old days!" He laughed at his cleverness.

"It's not as good as the real thing," he said. "But it beats flying around looking at flowers and mountaintops for eternity."

I hesitated.

"So what's your pleasure?" he asked again. "What have you been missin' the most? Good booze? Women? A friendly bar fight? I could even hook you up with some hard stuff if that's your thing—heroin, meth?" He laughed again.

I wanted to feel again, but was sickened at the thought of stalking people and preying on their emotional states. But these guys were not demons. They were partiers, drifters, and junkies. I felt above them, above this kind of activity, but could not shake the thought of trying it just a little.

"There's no harm in it," he assured me. "It's just a little fun. You take your ride until you get kicked out, and nobody's worse off for it."

"I don't know," I said. "To use someone like that. It doesn't seem right to mess with people in that way."

"I'll bet you did it when you were alive. It's just partying with friends. It's what we all did. The only difference is they don't know you're hanging with them."

"I'll think about it," I said.

"Hey, no rush, man. Just cruise with us for a while and see if it's your thing."

The more time I spent with my new friends, the more I matched their resonance. More beings—dim and lost souls wandering the Earth—came into view. I looked at them with pity and sometimes disgust. Meddling mothers followed their living children, approving and disapproving of their every decision. Broken-hearted lovers mournfully stalked their former loves. Men of importance still tried to assert their authority, arguing endlessly to unresponsive ears. Former gamblers loitered in casinos; alcoholics swarmed bars. I even saw religious spirits frequenting churches, angrily denouncing every form of perceived heresy, still pushing the pet doctrines they clung to in mortality.

I felt superior to them, but I didn't realize why they were becoming visible to me. I was one of them, drawn back, as with the force of gravity, to my old addictions. I saw them because I was like them.

At first I drifted with Raven and the gang and watched them at a distance. I was just curious, I told myself. I just wanted to see what they were up to. But soon it was not enough to observe; I was drawn into the games little by little, until one day Raven offered to let me hook into one of his old college friends. This ride was about beer and weed, two things I desperately missed.

"Maybe just a little," I said. "Just to see what it's like."

Raven grabbed my hand and in an instant we found ourselves in an upscale apartment in Phoenix. A pinkish twilight outlined rugged desert mountains in the distance. Floor to ceiling windows overlooked a city street lined with palm trees and trendy restaurants.

"Max, you old dog, you've done alright for yourself!" said Raven to a man on the couch who was unaware of our presence.

Max and a few others reclined around a coffee table littered with cans and ashes.

"This dude is crazy. Throws the wildest parties. We called him Mad Max in college. Everyone wanted to be his friend." Raven sat beside him.

"You got me my first hit of the hard stuff, didn't you Max. It's kinda your fault I'm here scraping up the leftovers while you live the good life." Raven's smile disappeared. "You knew when to quit and I didn't. So you're going to show my friend here a good time whether you want to or not."

Raven studied the protective glow of light surrounding the man's body. The light was like a living shield, swirling and pulsing with life.

Raven motioned for me to come closer.

"If you try to touch their body through the light, your arm will just sort of dissolve. It doesn't hurt, but you aren't really touching anything.

"But you see here," he said, pointing to the top of his friend's head. "This is the easiest place to enter a drunk." A halo of light above his head grew dimmer by the second. At the center the light thinned, almost forming an opening.

"I'll tell you when the time is right."

I felt ashamed standing next to Raven, like a child being shown something naughty by a rebellious older brother. But I also grew excited with anticipation. This was something new, something different, and I hungered to feel whatever this experience had to offer.

Max's friend challenged him to take a drag on a bowl of weed, and then chug a beer while holding the smoke in his lungs. The light at the crown of Max's head began to peel back, and Raven laughed as he focused on the thinning layer of light. He took me by one hand and reached into the open space with his other.

In a flash I was inside my host like a parasite injected into flesh. I hadn't realized just how much I had missed my body and its many pleasures. Oh how delicious to be drunk again—the numbness, the confusion, the carefree oblivion. Oddly, it was the feeling of not feeling, of numbing out, that I missed. The energy of my host brought back all sorts of memories from my party days.

My ride lasted for several days, as my host never allowed himself to get fully sober, maintaining at least a small buzz throughout the day. It ended when he had to sober up while visiting his parents. They were, unfortunately (as I thought at the time), good and loving people whose home was filled with laughter and light. While there, he stopped drinking and became unlivable; as light filled his being, his spirit fell out of resonance with mine and there was nothing to hold on to. His body expelled me.

For a short time I was ashamed of what I had done, how I had used another human being for my own pleasure. I thought of my guardian, that angel who rescued me from Hell. I wondered what he must think of me now, slumming with these new "friends." I must have been a waste of his time, a tremendous disappointment. I hoped he had forgotten me. I was where I belonged, and he was where he belonged.

The way to numb these thoughts now was the same as in my mortal life. I needed another fix. And my buddies generously offered me more. Most of my hosts were their old acquaintances, and some of them worked better than others.

"Sometimes they need a little nudge," said Raven. "You can't make them do anything, but you can help get them all worked up."

So I tried it, and it worked. *More*, I would tell them. *It's not enough yet. Keep going.* When it was over, I left and the host had to deal with the consequences.

Once again, I began to look at people as prey, coveting their bodies, stalking them, prodding them to indulge in some pleasure just so I could get my second-hand thrill.

I had been given the gift of escaping Hell, and now I was working my way back into it. This existence was less viscous, less hateful and vengeful, but still a Hell of addictions without satisfaction. We were junkies, using the bodies of others for our pleasure, encouraging darkness in them so we could gain access.

But such reflections about who I was becoming and how I had gotten there were drowned out by the desires of the moment. My descent was gradual as I experimented with new pleasures. Soon I needed my hosts to engage in harder and harder things to give me a thrill. I moved from drugs and alcohol to sexual perversions. Even violence, the intoxicating rush of domination, became an attractive possibility.

At first Raven and the gang generously offered me new hosts. But in time they started to hold back.

"You're taking more than your share," said Raven.

"I didn't think I was taking any more than anyone else."

"But that's the thing," he said. "You are taking and not giving. We're all friends here; we share. Your training is done, so your free-riding days are over."

I should have known the time was coming when I would have to pay up. I should have known that my friends' generosity wasn't without strings.

9

To keep Raven from rejecting me, I held back from taking more. But in time my cravings overcame me.

"I need something," I said. "Just a little to get me by."

Raven seemed pleased. "I can help with that, but you need to help us. It's time for you to bring your keg to the party, my man! Maybe you've noticed how we have special access to people we knew in life? You've noticed we don't just hook into random strangers, right? Everyone has earthly attachments. Those relationships are the lead, the access point."

He put his arm around my shoulder. "It's time for you to stop pretending you were unattached. You knew people. You can lead us to fresh bodies. Your friends and family can give us new experiences. You see, we're all feeling a little bored with the same ol' same ol'. The other problem is, I don't know how much longer we can protect you. Other gangs aren't as nice as us."

When I hesitated, his friendly, laid back demeanor turned serious and he pulled me toward him by my neck. The others surrounded me slowly, and I could see hunger in their eyes.

"You've been freeloading," said one of them. "It's time to party with *your* people."

They were hungry. They would have no excuses.

I had seen what spirit beings were capable of doing to one another. While the physical world was untouchable to us, we were not untouchable to each other, and we could cause each other real pain. A sense of dread overcame me. I had allowed myself to descend back into this kind of life.

All I had to do to keep their friendship was lead them to you, your girlfriend, your mother, my old friends, my old enemies, anyone I had some kind of resonance with in life. If I shared, then I would truly be part of the group that had given me my first sense of belonging since my death.

Unfortunately, I had long lost contact with my old party buddies and I couldn't have found them had I tried. My strongest connection was to you, my son, even if it wasn't a happy connection. I did not want to come after you but needed some time, something to distract them.

I convinced them that I had to go alone to scout and find the best prospects. They let me go; they were not afraid I would steal the hosts or run away. In a perverse way, I needed them and they needed me, and they knew it.

I dreaded the possibility of actually seeing you, so instead of going to you, I went to your home. I did not find you there, but I found your girlfriend. She was surrounded by layers of sadness. Heavy energy blanketed her like a cloud. You had been fighting again, and she was rehearsing in her mind the hurtful words that were spoken and what she would have said in return had she been thinking straight. I could see images in her energy. Thought-forms lingering from your argument surrounded her like a slow-moving whirlwind.

Even so, she was surrounded by a strong, protective casing of light. In the "best" hosts, these protective fields were weak or broken and easily penetrated. In the least promising hosts, they repelled us.

I was puzzled by how her field could be so strong, so untouchable, until I saw a thought-form hovering near her heart, not a memory, but a thought yet to be realized. It was the image of her cuddling a child, a baby yet unborn.

Hell was a distant memory by now, more like the memory of a bad dream than something I had actually experienced. But I remembered the words you rehearsed, the thing that troubled you so much as I listened to you. You said you were not ready to be a father.

I was not looking at the light of just one being, but two. For within her womb glowed the soul of a baby girl. Not just a baby girl. I saw her for what she was, felt the soul connection between us. This was my granddaughter.

In the presence of this innocence and purity, I became ashamed of what I was doing there, disgusted with what I had become again. Not all of Hell could have forced me to harm these beautiful beings. I wanted to protect them, and I tried to think of a way to hide them from the gang who eagerly awaited my return. But it was too late for that. I should have known they would follow me, that I had already formed a strong bond with them that led them to me like a homing beacon.

She was too bright for them. She was nearly untouchable, though perhaps they could cause her some annoyance, darken her mood even more. Now that they had found your home, they had an entry point into your life.

But they still needed me. I had the key to the souls I had known in life. I would have to be their channel, their conduit. Through me, they could learn weaknesses, desires, and points of entry. If I were gone, they would be powerless, or at least severely limited.

They came with their ready-to-party attitude, not so serious and threatening as before, but loud and rowdy. I told them this home had nothing for them, that it was a dead end, a waste of time.

"Well, let's have a look around first," Raven said, as they probed the new energetic landscape I had brought them into. "You aren't going soft on us are you, buddy?"

"I'm no good for new contacts," I said. Raven could feel my fear. "You might as well kick me out of the group, because I just don't know a lot of partiers.

The people I knew in life are too bright, too protected."

They howled with laughter.

"You don't end up going where you went when you died if your life was one big lovefest," said Raven. More laughter. They were smart and experienced. There was nothing I could say.

But I was still the key. They still needed me, and they knew it.

Raven became conciliatory. "Look, old man. It's just a little fun. You know that. No harm done. They still live their stupid little lives just like normal, no matter what we do."

But I knew that was not the case. We did damage to the hosts. We pulled them down. Maybe nothing as terrible as in Hell, but we helped spread filth by encouraging dark thoughts so we could keep the ride going.

As much as I had become addicted to Earth again, and as hard as it was to even think of leaving it, I knew I had to. I had to take my chances somewhere else. Who knew what possibilities were out there? I feared places that would be foreign and unfamiliar. My home planet had been such a relief to me, but I could see that staying there would bring me no good. As much as I thought I had the old life back, it was a lie. I did not belong there. I was grasping at something no longer meant for me. I was moving backward.

Raven knew he needed me and softened even more. He must have discerned my thoughts, my desire to run away. He told the gang to shut up and settle down.

"I'm sorry for barging in here like I own the

place," he said. "We can talk about this. If you aren't up for it yet, maybe we can wait. But let's at least just talk about it. Don't go getting all jumpy."

He was such a smooth talker, even nurturing. I wanted to believe him.

"Everyone has their own time, and maybe your time just isn't now. Either way, I hope we can still be friends."

I wanted to like him, and I wanted him to like me. He was the closest thing to a friend I had found since my death. There was my guardian, but he was on too high of a plane for me.

Raven had enough control over his emotions to get what he wanted. He knew how to say the right things, and now, I realized, he was merely stalling. Behind his easy-going façade, I saw hunger in his eyes. The longer I let them stay in the home, and the longer I let them talk and play with the idea, the more they could hack into my mind and spirit. If I waited too long, they wouldn't need me. They would have the frequencies and resonances to do their work.

I needed help. I would not call upon God, or even my guardian, for I felt beneath their contempt, having botched my first rescue. But I needed someone. I remembered the woman who visited me. I would not ask her to get involved in this mess, but I remembered her last words, that when the student was ready, the teacher would appear.

I had chosen my teacher in the form of Raven, and it landed me in the gutter. I looked deep within to find the teacher I wanted. Who could help me out of this insanity? I recalled my time at college, when I finally decided to stop partying and take my education seriously. I remembered how, just briefly, I had experienced the joy of higher learning. I remembered gaining a love for factual, rational knowledge. That was the time in my life that I first experienced some semblance of stability. College was a refuge from the irrational ups and downs of my father's view of life.

I had learned of a universe governed by facts, not emotions. I had learned of a predictable universe of laws and order—a universe that did not need God or gods, or angels, or demons. It was a universe that could be measured and understood. That was the learning I wanted.

I let this memory work in me. I was willing to leave the familiarity of Earth if I could live in such a mindset again. I let this desire grow inside me until I felt the familiar, magnetic pull of my heart. I felt the happiness of that time and felt myself lifting, getting lighter as Raven and the others slowly began to fade.

Raven saw what I was doing, that I was trying to escape, and his soft, easygoing countenance turned to rage. He grasped at me but by then I was already dissolving. They would not have access to you or your family, and they knew it. They had failed, and I was drawn upward, rising, not with speed and power as I did in the grasp of my angels, but still moving upward. The atmosphere lightened, and again I had the sensation of something lifting from my chest, allowing me to breathe again. I had fallen so gradually, only lifting out of the hazy energies revealed the contrast.

I entered a tunnel that branched in countless directions, but I did not need to make choices about where to go. My heart led me, and when I arrived, I knew I was in the right place.

10

I found myself in a grove of giant trees, ancient trees. They stood like sentinels, like magnificent beings that had observed the comings and goings of this realm for eons. Sunlight streamed down through their canopy, illuminating varieties of plants and flowers I had never known on Earth. I walked along a sandy pathway that led from the grove and opened into a clearing, where I saw green hills rolling into the horizon. In the distance I saw the outline of a city.

A gentle breeze moved the tall grasses, fragrant with the warmth of a summer day. I breathed in the lightness of the atmosphere and felt something unfamiliar—peace. As a spirit on Earth I had felt intrigue, curiosity, desires, and appetites, but never peace.

I had no desire to fly around, as I had when I first returned to Earth. Simply walking down the path was enough. Every step was a pleasure. I did not know where I was going, or why I was walking, only that it felt good to walk, to be going somewhere, so I kept on.

In the distance, I saw a man sitting on a bench near the path. He was reading a book. He wore a neatly trimmed beard, gray collared shirt unbuttoned at the top, and a black sports coat.

As I drew closer, I recognized him immediately. He was one of my favorite professors in college. His class was the one that helped me stop partying and hit the books. He taught me the joy of "the life of the mind," as he always put it—the pleasure of thinking, of learning, of discovering the observable world.

I didn't recall a lot from his class, but I did remember how empowered I felt upon discovering what he called an empirically discernible universe. It was the perfect antidote to the inconsistent religious convictions of my father, who, I felt at the time, used religion as just another tool of domination.

Although he was old and frail when I knew him— still teaching the class as a kind of retirement hobby— his mind was precise and sharp and didn't allow for "fuzzy thinking."

He was widely published and well-respected in his field, a fact he did not hide from us. In class, he did not give praise easily, but when he did, I relished it. Impressing him with my own budding intellect became an all-consuming quest during that pivotal semester. I wrote my papers with great care, imagining how he would receive every line. I tried to use the words and terms that he used in ways I felt he would use them, and just using these words made me feel powerful and smart.

Even when I took issue with an idea from one of the philosophers we were studying, it was only in ways

I felt he would approve of. My goal was not to get an A. That was too easy in a class of uninterested freshmen fulfilling general requirements. My greatest desire was that he would like me and think of me as a promising intellectual.

Now, seeing him in the afterlife, I wondered if I had somehow conjured him up in my imagination. Was this some kind of apparition to comfort me after my escape from Raven? But this was no mistake; he was as real as anything or anyone I had seen. I approached him casually, not sure whether to stop and acknowledge him or to keep on my way. He was not the aging, gray-haired professor I remembered, but a young and handsome man. Yet I had no doubt it was him. As I drew closer, I felt the old nervousness I always felt around him when I was in college, the anxiety that I would say or do something stupid.

"It never ceases to amaze me," he said, not looking up from his book, "how the right people from the old world just sort of show up at the right place and time."

I was flattered that he thought of me as "the right people."

He closed his book and looked at me with the casual, confident gaze I remembered from college, a look that said, "Yes, I've already thought of that," and you could bet he had. Nothing you could say, no argument you could produce, would unsettle him. But he was not mean; he was a gentleman-scholar. His dignified presence provided a welcome relief from the company of drifters and partiers I had just escaped on Earth.

"I'm not surprised I was led here," I said. "Your class changed my…" I was afraid to say it. He had an aversion to sentimentality. "I loved my class with you."

"Well, there are plenty of slums in the universe. Certainly worse places you could have gone than here," he said.

"I *know*," I said, with more conviction than I intended. He looked at me curiously until I asked, "But where is 'here'?"

"That's a much more complicated question than you might imagine, one that our theoretical physicists could better answer than I," he said. "In a sense, you aren't even in the same universe as the old world, but in another sense, the old world is right here. You are in another dimension on the same planet. But this dimension has the finest institutions of higher learning that I have encountered. I consider myself fortunate to have been welcomed here."

"These are just the Gateways," he continued, "where we keep an eye out for new arrivals. I am taking my rotation on the recruitment committee, looking for promising talent. If I remember correctly, you showed much potential as an undergraduate."

It felt good to be recognized and accepted by one I had known on Earth. I wanted to join whatever he was offering admission to, and he knew it.

"Compared to where I've been, this world seems like Heaven."

"Well, I don't care for the term *Heaven*," he said. "But where have you been?"

I hesitated, embarrassed at my recent history,

ashamed to admit how easily I had been led into what he called the slums of the universe.

"I don't know what to call it. Let's just say I fell in with the wrong crowd."

"I think you'll find this place more agreeable," he said. "The people who come here come ready to learn. Sometimes they come from lower realms; sometimes they come straight from Earth. Either way, it's a kind of refuge in what, by all accounts, is a pretty hostile universe. In any case, it's the only place trying to discover what's going on in the cosmos in a professional and rational manner. And that's what brings me out here to the portal, recruiting for the University. If you choose, you can be admitted on a provisional basis to assess your academic potential. Once fully admitted, you select your discipline of study and advance through the various degrees, eventually teaching new arrivals."

"A university," I said, trying to conceal my excitement. "I have missed my college days. I like the sound of it."

Here was an opportunity I once longed for on Earth. In my life I seriously considered a career in academia, eventually deciding against it and choosing a more lucrative job in business instead, a choice I regretted my whole life. As my business career ground my soul into the dirt, I daydreamed about what it might have been like to be a professor on a quiet campus.

"You need to understand, life at the University is not just a big picnic. It takes work, but it can be very rewarding. So, what do you think? Do you want to join or take your chances elsewhere?"

Before I could utter the words, my heart answered the question, and we found ourselves standing in a small park, surrounded by beautiful buildings.

"That's what I love about traveling in the holographic universe," he chuckled. "Sometimes it knows what we want before we do."

A network of stone pathways connected stately buildings of every architectural design imaginable. Some looked like what you'd find in an old European city, while others resembled nothing I had ever seen on Earth. Parkways with ponds and streams and foot bridges separated the buildings. Students sat on benches under prehistoric looking trees studying books on what appeared to be sheets of glass.

"Welcome to the campus," he said. "Well, at least part of it. It's enormous. I've only seen a fraction in all my time here."

He took me on a quick tour of a few of the departments, a kind of freshman orientation. We passed large lecture halls where students looked on earnestly as professors pointed to screens. Other rooms were filled with scientific equipment more sophisticated than anything I had seen on Earth. A quiet and orderly atmosphere pervaded the campus.

"I will be your mentor at first," he said. "But in time you may choose others as your research interests take shape. But I was wondering if you could help me with something right away. In my introductory philosophy class we're talking about the meaning of a multilayered, multidimensional universe. It sounds like you've seen more than your share of it. I find the slum worlds fascinating, personally, and I know my students would like to hear your story."

I shuddered at the thought. I wanted to put those experiences behind me, not become the campus freak show. But he was asking a favor, and I couldn't let him down.

"I can talk about what I know," I said. "But I don't really understand it myself—where I've been, I mean."

"That's why you're here, my friend. We will help you."

11

More than a hundred students looked on as the professor introduced me to the class. Even a few faculty members had dropped in to hear my tale.

"Begin with the moment of your death on Earth," he said, then he sat at a nearby desk.

I told my story, and whenever he felt I was sugar coating things, he pressed me for detail.

"Few of us have been to the darker dimensions," he said. "The more you can tell us, the better."

Despite his prodding, I left out much of my experience in Hell and on Earth, not wanting to relive the horrors. Also, I didn't want to feel like an ex-convict warning school children to just say no to drugs.

When I came to my rescue, I nearly used the word "angels" to describe my guardian and his attendants but knew the term would not be well received in this environment. So I told them "beings of light" came to my rescue.

"It looks like you have met the Shiners," said the professor with a laugh. "They must be getting desperate if they're milling around in the slums to look for new recruits." The students chuckled.

"Shiners?" I said, surprised that he had used the same term as Raven.

"They're part of a powerful religious cult. They live in a different realm, but they come here looking for new recruits, luring gullible people with the promise of a better life in a better world. Basically the same kind of religious garbage that was sold in the old life. Those who were most religious during their life on Earth are the most susceptible to their evangelizing. But at least you didn't get sucked in, to your credit."

"But they helped me," I said. "They were there when I needed them."

"Sure, they'll help you as long as you buy into what they're selling," said the professor.

"But what *about* religion and God and all that?"

It was a risk to go there. Whenever religion came up in class in the old world, he would put on a mock attitude of patience and restraint, as if, were he less of a gentleman, he would be tempted to let loose a tirade and put such nonsense to rest immediately, but would instead patiently explain just one more time the folly of the student's question. Most of the students learned what kinds of questions to ask and what kinds not to ask.

"I mean," I continued, "here we are, still alive after our death on Earth. Weren't they wrong, the atheists—or what did you call them—the scientific materialists? Didn't they get it wrong?"

The class looked at me with a mixture of humor and anticipation, as if to say, *this is going to be good.*

"The materialists were wrong?" replied the professor with mock surprise. He leaned back and folded his arms. "Well let's think about that. Look around and tell me what you see. If it's not matter and energy, tell me what it is. Touch your face. Are you a ghost? A dream?"

"But we're still alive after our death," I said, trying to recover. "Doesn't that mean we must have souls or something like that?" I was unguarded. These questions, unlike those I asked in college, were sincere, born of genuine confusion rather than a desire to sound smart. "You told me yourself that the afterlife was a construct to pacify the uneducated and oppressed, to keep them from revolting and trying to improve their life on Earth."

"Well," he said. "I was both right and wrong, just as you are at this moment. Yes, consciousness somehow continues, and we have some excellent theories to explain the physics behind it. The mind and body we developed on Earth somehow forms a copy of itself in a parallel dimension. When one body dies, the other continues in the parallel dimension. Many papers have been written about this. No need to call this copy a 'soul' or conclude that it's eternal or comes from God. It's just the laws of quantum physics playing out, no grand design or intention."

"But there might be something more going on here," I said.

He only laughed. "You're new here. You don't understand how far we've come in our understanding of the universe. Where is this Heaven that 'might' exist? Where is that God who sits on His golden throne answering everyone's questions and solving everyone's problems? Nowhere to be found. No harps or angels or Jesus to make it all better.

"We still answer our own questions and solve our own problems through scientific inquiry. Our research continues to point to a rational, natural universe, although admittedly more layered and complex than we realized on Earth. When you dig deeper into nature, you don't find super-nature. You just find more nature, matter and energy just like before. Our knowledge is still empirical, observable, and repeatable. The scientific method applies here as much as it did in the old life, even more."

I recognized the old fire and certainty in his voice, a mixture of defiance and intelligence. Just listening to him made me want to be on his side. His tone dared you to disagree with him.

"Besides," he continued. "How certain are you that you are experiencing life after your death on Earth?"

"I died in a car wreck," I said.

"Can you be quite certain of that? What evidence do you have of your physical death?"

This was another of his techniques I remembered from college. It was one I loved very much, especially when he applied it to what I thought of as less-intelligent students. He had a way of taking the most certain and obvious truths of our existence and turning them into problems. He could make someone doubt the very ground they walked upon.

I didn't know how to answer. My existence was as real and obvious to me as anything I had known. I had a perfect recollection of all that had happened to me since my car wreck. But I had not, come to think of it, actually seen my dead body. I had not seen my funeral. Most of my post-death memories, though vivid, were more like a nightmare.

He let me puzzle over the question for a moment, then continued.

"There is a school of thought among some of our best minds here that asserts all of this is a dream. They believe their physical death has not actually occurred and that this is a coma-induced dream world. They believe their bodies are on life support in hospitals, and that eventually they will awaken back into their regular life, or their family will pull the plug, finally extinguishing their existence.

"Can you prove they are wrong? Can you prove to them they exist? Can you prove that you exist as a real entity beyond your supposed physical death on Earth? Maybe you survived that car wreck and you're in a hospital right now, hooked up to life support."

My mind was spinning, and I felt dizzy, like there was nothing to grasp on to. The thing I thought most certain—that my life had continued—was now in question. I could hear other students chuckling under their breath. Now I was the class dunce, paying the price for having said something stupid.

I was about to attempt Descartes's famous "I think therefore I am" proposition, but I knew he had already thought of that and would have a ready response. I was done talking and wanted to dissolve into the anonymity of the class. If I was, in fact, in a coma somewhere, this would have been a great time for someone to pull the plug.

"I guess I can't prove it," I said, finally breaking the silence.

And then it came, the rescue, the counterargument that would show the issue was more complex than originally supposed. He wasn't without mercy. He would hold students intellectually hostage, but he would eventually throw them a bone.

"The problem with that theory, of course, is that everyone who holds it believes they are the ones lying in the hospital bed in a coma, and that the rest of us are just props in their dream. To my mind, this is bad philosophy. We only have access to our own consciousness so it follows that we will be biased in favoring the reality of our own existence above others. We must take the facts as they are, and not fall into a solipsistic denial of reality on the one hand, or, on the other hand, strive for a supposed absolute reality in God."

I was relieved, not only because he was moving on from my interrogation, but because assuming the reality of my existence was not as stupid as he first made it sound. Now I can see the only stupid thing I had done was to give him power to invalidate my own experience. I allowed him to dictate the only acceptable ways to pursue truth.

Now that I had been made a fool by his intellect, I decided never to be caught off guard again. I would redeem myself. He would see in me the intelligence he had once appreciated. I had grown intellectually soft after college, and even after my death my mind had dulled. I would work and prove myself again, and he would not regret taking me in. I wanted him to see me as a peer worthy of real debate.

After the class, the professor approached me and said, "I hope I didn't come off as too harsh. I appreciate you having the guts to tell your story. You're lucky you made it, you know. And I don't just mean out of that pit. It looks like the Shiners are on to you, so you aren't in the clear yet. Don't let them get into your mind."

I wasn't worried. I had found a new home and wasn't looking for another. The University captured my imagination, and I felt like I could spend eons there. But the professor knew me better than I knew myself. I had been infected with the God virus, as he once called it, and my symptoms were already showing.

12

From that moment on, I committed myself to studying and preparing for full admission into one of the more prestigious colleges. I seriously considered the sciences and the joy of dealing with factual knowledge and experimentation. I wanted to know how the universe worked and what new things science had discovered in this world.

But I wanted more than mere factual knowledge about the physical universe. I wanted to understand what had happened to me since my death. The continuation of my life was both mysterious and unsettling. On Earth the question of how to live the good life, the right life, only affected a handful of decades before it stopped mattering. Now the consequences reached far into an unknown future. So I was, to the satisfaction of my professor, drawn to philosophy.

I studied deeply and earnestly. In time, I learned

the university system, how to gain awards and recognition and achieve new levels of advancement. When I reached higher levels I was draped in ceremonial clothing and presented with a colored sash, each color indicating some achievement.

When the time came for me to apply to a college, my professor called me to his office. He was highly ranked in his department and had earned a spacious corner office overlooking a courtyard lined with trees and fountains. On one of the walls hung a display of several silken sashes that glistened in the light. They were of a higher quality and richer color than anything students received.

I sat as he finished reading a student's paper.

"It's time for you to choose a specialized college," he said, not looking up from the paper. "You've had some time to explore and think about your interests."

"Yes. I was thinking about philosophy."

"Excellent choice!" he said. "Though I am a little biased. What branch?"

"I was thinking…philosophy of religion. Maybe something like theology."

The professor sighed and turned toward the window, as if he couldn't look me in the eyes.

"Well, there are schools that do that sort of thing, none of them well-respected. I'll be honest; it seems like a waste of genuine academic potential."

"I want to make sense of my experience since my death," I said. "I need to understand what happened to me, what's going on here."

"And you think theology will provide answers?"

"It might."

"Reading Saint Augustine is going to tell you what happened to you in the slums?"

"I could do field work. Explore other realms or other planets."

"Field work!" he laughed and shook his head in disbelief. "You would never make it back. I've known good people who've left the safety of campus and never made it back. They might have even ended up in the hole you crawled out of. You have an opportunity here, a safe and stable career in an otherwise chaotic and, frankly, dangerous universe, and you come to me talking about God and exploring other worlds. Nobody with any brains ventures far from campus. You of all people should know better, considering where you came from."

He turned to the window again and stroked his beard.

"Smart people have driven themselves insane looking for final answers," he continued. "I've known promising minds who left their positions and ended up nowhere, all in a quest to find some elusive thing called truth. You want to know what truth is? This office is truth. Tonight I will be recognized for my contribution to gender studies in post-existentialist thought. I am widely regarded as the preeminent expert in that emerging field. *That* is truth. Other scholars cite me in their own research now. It's the product of hard work and focus."

I was already regretting my decision. Maybe I hadn't thought it through enough. With the professor, I felt like I didn't think about anything enough.

He continued, "I've taken a liking to you, maybe

from our association in the old life. So I'm going to give you some advice. If you want to make it around here, you've got to stop dabbling in so many subjects and become an expert. You know just enough about different subjects to never make a real contribution. And you'd get eaten alive in a debate. Carve out your niche. Find something that nobody else cares about and become an expert in it. It's your place of retreat. It's safety; it's home. You'll always have the upper hand, at least in that one little area. You can build a career on that bit of turf. If you keep pursuing this God stuff, I cannot give you a recommendation in good conscience."

"I guess I didn't realize that much was at stake," I said.

"Even more," he said. "Students who show too much interest in God are sometimes recommended for remediation. We delicately refer to them as developing intellects. And you are not a developing intellect.

"I probably shouldn't tell you this, and I can't guarantee anything." He paused as if deliberating. "There's been talk of you receiving the Purple Sash."

I was breathless. "The Purple Sash? But I'm so new here."

"That's my point," he said. "I think you'd be the newest arrival to get it. And it would position you perfectly to apply to some of the prestigious colleges."

I had no idea the Purple Sash was even a consideration. I shuddered to think I had almost thrown my study away on some intellectual hobby. I thought I only stood out as a curiosity, the guy who came from Hell. Some students even seemed nervous around me, like I was capable of violence. But now I was being recognized for my mind.

I knew now the professor had my back. He wanted me to succeed. It was rare to have an advocate like him on campus. I thanked him for his time and told him I would reconsider my interests.

I once again immersed myself in study and settled into the safe and comforting routine of campus life. I made friends, met new teachers, and attended seminars presented by some of the great minds of Earth's history. On the surface we presented a genteel air, but just beneath we competed ruthlessly to get to the top. Our ability was always on display, and even casual conversations provided opportunity for intellectual jousting. The first and highest goal was to avoid embarrassing one's self, an objective best accomplished by showing only polite interest in others' studies and not asking too many questions.

The most horrifying thing, the terror that held me—and I suppose others—hostage, was the feeling that at some point I would be discovered as a fraud, a phony, a hack who did not belong in the prestigious halls of the University. Even the highest professors feared venturing beyond the boundaries of their expertise.

I entered my studies hoping to explore big and bold ideas, to find answers to the kind of questions the professor taught us to ask in the old life. But the most interesting conversation I had was when the professor questioned the reality of my existence. At least that conversation pointed somewhere, addressed my actual concerns. With each new advancement, instead of opening to new possibilities, my field of study became narrower, and I was less free to discuss big questions.

But my studies in philosophy and science led me again and again to these questions—God and of meaning. As much as I wanted the Purple Sash, I could not turn away from these problems. Unlike many of the comfortable souls around me, I had experienced in Hell and in the form of my guardian some of the worst and the best the universe had to offer. Nothing in my studies explained my experience.

I decided to study in secret, slipping into the rarely used theological section of the library. The grand scale of the library made me feel small by comparison. Tall marble columns supported vaulted ceilings, and ornate windows several stories high let in columns of golden light. Like a medieval monk, I spent countless days pouring over theological treatise and the study of comparative religion. Some of the books were texts from the old world that had been transcribed from memory, but most were dissertations and publications written by professors in this realm. The more I searched for answers, the more confused I became. But I felt I was at least asking the right questions now.

Students studied quietly. Absorbed in their own work, no one paid much attention to others. That is why when one day a woman glanced furtively in my direction, I began to worry. Her interest was unnerving. We were alone in the theology stacks. I considered portaling away, but that would have seemed too much like running, and I wanted to know who she was and why she watched me.

13

Soon she approached me and said, "It looks like you're interested in theology. I also like learning about God."

I cringed.

"Well, I don't," I lied. "I'm just doing a little research for a project."

I continued scanning the shelves without looking at her. I didn't want anyone to see us talking. It occurred to me that she could be a spy for the college. Had they found out about my alternative studies? Or was she a Shiner looking for new recruits in the comparative religion section of the library? If she was, I couldn't risk being seen with her.

"There are perspectives about God and the universe that aren't covered in these books," she said. "Maybe I could help you out."

I felt humiliated and looked around again to make sure no one saw us talking.

"You can help by not distracting me," I said,

pretending to be absorbed in a book.

"When the student is ready…" she said.

I now recognized her voice, but when I looked up she was gone, having vanished in a flash of light. Why was this woman following me? Was she one of those Shiners, trying to sign me up for their program? Had my guardian sent her, not ready to give up? I was beginning to feel watched and uneasy, like unseen forces were conspiring.

My curiosity about religious matters grew stronger. Were these Shiners on to something? Professors, and their student imitators, spoke of them with such derision on campus that I could hardly consider the possibility. Even the respectable theologians dismissed them. Part of me still refused to believe my rescuers were Shiners, mere evangelizing cultists.

I tried to forget this encounter and continue my research. After the sparsely populated shelves of the theology section of the library yielded all they had to offer, I resolved to spend some time in the theological schools themselves. These schools sat on the periphery of campus and were relatively small departments, compared to the rest. Rising students only considered this line of study when more serious programs had rejected them.

To keep my professor from getting suspicious, I invented a pretext for my visit to that side of campus. I told him I was working on a paper tentatively titled, "Resurrecting Zeus: The post-existential persistence of adherence to religious mythologies." He wasn't entirely pleased with the topic, saying it sounded more like freshmen work, but approved of my general direction. When I told him I would have to visit the theological schools, he warned me, only half-jokingly, about "growing dumber" through my research.

The architecture on that side of campus was different from the other buildings, bearing a distinctly religious appearance—Cathedrals, Buddhist and Hindu temples, and even Greek and Roman temples but of a larger and more beautiful scale than anything on Earth. The buildings were not places of worship so much as tributes to the religious diversity of Earth. The people coming and going were dressed in clothing that must have matched the period in which each lived on Earth. I saw monks in robes and nuns in habits, as well as priests and preachers from various time periods.

I passed a Hindu temple with white granite steps. They led upward to ornate domes trimmed with golds and pastels. On the steps sat a Hindu swami draped in yellow ochre robes, absorbed in meditation in the lotus posture. I paused to look at him, believing he did not see me, as his eyes were closed.

"The divine consciousness sees all," he said, speaking directly to me without opening his eyes. I wasn't sure if he spoke with an Indian accent or if my own mind and expectations just interpreted his words that way.

"You are new to these parts; welcome to this little corner of the astral universe, just one little speck in God's cosmic dream."

"So, that's what's going on," I said with mock interest. "We're all dreaming."

"No," he laughed. "We're not all dreaming; we're

all *being* dreamed in the Divine Mind."

I had heard some of this before and wanted to see where it led.

"So that's why you meditate, right? To awaken?"

He didn't answer.

"I'm doing a little research on what people believed on Earth. I take it you were a Hindu. Do you still consider yourself a Hindu?"

"A meaningless label assigned by a colonial power. It means nothing to me, but if you insist, then yes, something like a Hindu, bound in yoga with God."

"Then you believe in God?"

"Yes, I still believe in God. That is precisely the problem and why I await my next incarnation. I believe, but have not become. I have not yet realized God within. A Self-realized master does not *believe*, but *is*. Belief must die. I wait on this most pleasant astral planet until I am reborn into the material universe."

"Self-realized? You mean finding yourself, true spirit? But aren't we spirits now? Didn't we leave our physical bodies back on Earth?"

"This astral body is no more your true self than the physical animal you left in the grave. You have brought your ego with you, you know. It doesn't die so easily as the physical body. You died, but you didn't die enough. You need to die some more."

"Die some more?"

"Any part of you that does not realize its oneness with God must die. The god within patiently awaits your awakening. Your physical death was just moving into a different landscape. You have a lot more dying to do, so you had better get started."

With this he closed his eyes again and said, "Can you hear it?"

I listened but could hear nothing.

"The Om vibration creates and sustains the universe."

I listened intently but could only hear the regular hum of campus life—people talking, doors opening and closing, and church bells ringing in the distance.

The yogi drew a large breath and let out a deep "Ommmmm" that lasted several seconds. I looked around, a little embarrassed, and slipped away quietly.

I was drawn to an amphitheater where a small crowd was forming. On the stage, two professors sat across a table from two relaxed and casually dressed people who looked somehow foreign.

"What is this?" I asked a young man next to me.

"Well, it might be a debate, if the Shiners don't scare off too soon. They come here a lot, but don't stick around very long."

All doubts were now resolved. These Shiners, who looked naively cheerful, had nothing in common with my rescuers. They seemed young and vulnerable next to the learned professors of religion.

The professors pelted the Shiners with a series of questions, making reference to the works of famous theologians, works the Shiners did not appear to know or have any interest in.

"This isn't Heaven," said one of the Shiners. "There are worlds above this one."

"And where is your evidence? In which text are you basing this claim?" said a professor.

"The text of experience. You will need to come and see. Leave the familiarity of this place for just a little while and decide for yourself."

"This is how it always ends," said a professor to the gathering crowd. "They cannot withstand the heat of rational debate and instead invite me on one of their little field trips." The audience laughed.

There was no chance the professor would accept their offer. It was common knowledge that this world was among the finest that a soul could hope to live in. Rumors and horror stories about gullible souls getting lured into dark corners of the universe circulated, probably coming from people like me. This planet was an island of tranquility, and even with its intellectual rivalries, was far more peaceful than Earth. We felt lucky to be here and considered ourselves part of an elite society.

Those who went with the Shiners, as many souls did, never came back. Only wild speculation about brainwashing and abuse explained their absence. As predicted, the debate ended rather quickly when, having reached an impasse on the question of visiting another place, the Shiners disappeared without further argument.

I spent days listening in on every debate and discussion I could fit into my schedule. The scholars and students in these religious schools were not the dreamy, simple-minded folks my professor had made them out to be. They were intelligent, curious, and driven by sincerity not common in my own college. Where my own philosophy department had given up on the idea of ultimate truth, these folks still believed they could discover something important or arrive at a better understanding of the universe.

I met students and professors from every religion imaginable—Catholics, Protestants, Muslims, Jews. Even some of the smaller sects—Jehovah's Witnesses, Mormons, and Seventh-day Adventists were all amply represented. And there were no dead faiths. I talked to Zoroastrians, disciples of Hermes, Manicheans, Neo-Platonists. Religions that had cultivated traditions of intellectual debate were disproportionately represented, but I do not doubt that had I looked longer, I would have found medicine men and tribal shamans. Forms of all these religions were practiced throughout the smaller villages and cities on the planet, but these theological schools and seminaries were the intellectual center. For the most part, the various faiths maintained a respectful relationship, a kind of polite distance.

Many who came here upon their death experienced an initial disappointment at not having their doctrinal convictions validated once and for all. But it didn't take them long to jump back into the old game. Soon they found themselves staking out positions and defending favorite doctrines. Most of them believed that in doing so, they were engaging in God's work—a work they had started in their mortal life and had only to complete here.

Sometimes intense debates gathered large audiences. Even the Shiners, whom I scrupulously avoided, were in on the action, not in the debates, but working the curious onlookers on the edge of the crowd.

This was religion as I remembered it, a bottomless pit of beliefs and claims and counterclaims. Sacred texts were used as weapons to prove and disprove points of doctrine. There were factions, break-offs of those factions, and break-offs of the break-offs. Every week it seemed a new group would form around some speculative idea or charismatic speaker.

I became depressed and disillusioned, and my professor could see my studies were suffering.

"I warned you," he said one day. "Nothing interferes more with good academic work than dabbling in that metaphysical nonsense. You need to come back to real intellectual work."

I tried, but no matter what I studied, I was left feeling empty, hungry. My thoughts kept returning to the so-called Shiners and their invitation to see other possibilities. The idea was absurd, especially considering what I had been through. Leaving this peaceful realm would have been insane. But perhaps because I had seen the worst, I was a little less afraid than the others. I had been through Hell and felt, in a small way, stronger and wiser.

Something drew me to the Shiners, perhaps just a hope for something new. The "real" intellectual work my professor would have me resume filled me with dread and boredom. Having been trapped in lower worlds before, I knew a dead end when I saw one, and life at the University, while far better than anything I had experienced, wrapped itself around my soul with suffocating tedium. I decided it was time to take a chance and see what these zealots had to offer.

14

Now that I had become known as a disinterested researcher, I was largely ignored at the theological schools. The Shiners no longer approached me, so, embarrassingly, I would have to approach them. They would be excited to have someone show unsolicited interest in their message, especially one of my rank.

I found some at the edge of a large crowd, listening to a debate between a notable Greek philosopher and a fifth century Catholic monk. It wasn't difficult to find them because they were paying no attention to the debate. Instead they scanned the audience, as if reading the eyes of the listeners.

I approached a woman whose youth and attractiveness I mistook for naive innocence.

"So…" I said, suddenly aware that I wasn't sure how to start the conversation. "Are you one of the

'Shiner' people?"

"You tell me. Do I look shiny?" she asked. Her humor was disarming and put me at ease. Maybe these were normal people after all.

"I have a few questions about your organization," I said. "But just for research purposes. You should understand I'm not interested in joining anything. I'd just like to know what you are up to, what ideas you offer lost souls."

"Sure, we can talk," she said, with less enthusiasm than I expected.

"But we can't talk here," I said. "It has to be somewhere out of town, alone."

"Well, we'll have to see what we can arrange," she said, looking into the distance as if uncertain about how to proceed. She seemed almost indifferent to my curiosity.

"Wait a minute. I'm showing some interest in your...uh...organization here. I thought you'd be happy to have a potential customer. I thought all you guys wanted was new recruits."

"Only when they are ready," she said.

"Am I ready?" I didn't want to appear earnest and maintained a skeptical, amused distance.

"How should I know? Only you can know that."

"But don't you want me to become a Shiner?"

"We prefer the term messenger. It's just more accurate."

"If you are a messenger, then what's your message?" I had hoped for a ready-made sales pitch.

"It's different for everyone," she said.

"How do you decide who gets what message?"

"I don't. They don't come from me. They come from the organization. I just help out. And if you don't mind, I had better be on my way."

"But don't you have a message for me?" I said, reaching for her arm. I had now revealed my hand. I was desperate. She could see I was not merely curious and amused.

She relaxed and smiled, as if pleased she had elicited something honest from me. She looked into my eyes. I would have been uncomfortable except that her gaze was beautiful, and she was not looking at me, but into me. She then looked into the distance, as if communicating with someone else.

I looked over my shoulder to see who she was talking to. Though I had at first judged her as normal, I now reconsidered.

Her countenance broke into a gentle and knowing smile. She turned to me again and said, "Here is your message: *The truth is in the grove.*"

She began to leave, but I wanted to ask more questions.

"But wait…"

"You have received a message; now you have a choice."

I knew immediately what she meant by the grove, but wasn't sure how she knew. Some distance out of town, not far from the Gateways where I arrived, I had been drawn to a large grove of trees, several acres. The trees in this grove seemed different, more ancient than the rest, and were of a species I had never seen on Earth.

There were no walkways through the forest and

therefore no other visitors. The University was not a realm of adventurers; the academics did not stray from well-trodden paths. It was one of the few places I could go to truly be alone.

It was some time before my schedule opened up for a visit to the grove. I arrived in the evening. I expected my new messenger to be waiting for me and that we would somehow find one another. The Shiners had a way of keeping track of prospective recruits. It added to the mystique that fooled some of the lesser souls among us.

I wondered if perhaps this grove, remote and secluded, was a secret meeting place for the Shiners, but there was no evidence that anyone else had ever been there. I waited for a while, but could find no one. I called out. I searched every part of the grove, one end to the other. I finally left, irritated and offended. Had I been sent on a wild goose chase? Was this their idea of a joke? It seemed that this was no way to treat a potential convert, not that I considered myself such, but they didn't know that.

I returned every day, waiting for some kind of meeting, some kind of encounter, but nothing. I went back to the theological schools and looked for my Shiner, but she was nowhere to be found. The others said they had no message for me, and that if I had received a message, I would not receive more until the first had been understood.

"The grove is empty!" I insisted, but they only smiled and continued their business.

I was surprised they garnered as many followers as they had, given these lousy sales tactics. I assumed they didn't know who I was. Even though my rank was still relatively low, it was much higher than their usual prospects. I thought they should have been honored that I took them seriously, probably the first of my academic standing to have done so.

I returned to the grove daily, telling myself it was just for evening walks, but I looked in all directions for any sign of my messenger.

The truth is in the grove. The words repeated in my mind again and again, like a mantra.

When I told my professor of my encounter, as a kind of funny anecdote, he became serious. He said it was time my research move in more productive directions.

"Don't let them get inside your head," he warned. "You won't be able to think straight."

And he was right. My studies became impossible. The only thing on my mind was the message, repeating itself, begging to be answered. When she delivered it, she spoke the words into my soul. It was written within me, and I could not have forgotten it even if I had tried.

The grove became my obsession. I now spent every spare moment searching for a clue, a secret message. If the grove contained the truth, I would find it, even if it meant going mad. In time I skipped classes and eventually withdrew from my college.

I walked up and down the large expanse of trees, sometimes calling out for a response, sometimes turning over rocks or studying leaves for patterns. I considered every possibility. Perhaps the stones on the ground were arranged in a certain way. Perhaps the trees themselves formed a meaningful pattern. Maybe the truth was buried in the ground. Soon the grove was dotted with mounds of dirt where I had dug holes.

In the library I searched for books on the history of the grove, looking for anything significant about its past. But nothing turned up. It barely registered on maps and was of no interest to the geography professors.

The grove held a secret I could not see, something I was not clever enough to discover. My messenger left me a puzzle, and I couldn't solve it. Was this where God would meet me? What about the angels who rescued me from Hell? I cried out to God. If he was there, would he please, please, reveal the truth of the grove to me. I begged and pleaded, but was answered only with silence.

I then dispensed with my politeness, became the serious intellectual, and reasoned that it appeared that He, or someone, had been after me for quite some time, and now here I was. Here was their big chance. I was ready to be taught, and, according to what I had been told, the teacher should appear. So this was the time to appear because if it didn't happen, I was leaving the grove forever.

Only silence.

But I couldn't leave.

I constructed theories about why I had been called to the grove. The truth was in the grove, and it was a quiet place to think. Perhaps I was expected to discover truth with the power of my own mind. There, in the quiet of the grove, I was to apply my mind to the problems I had been secretly pondering. That was it.

God expected me to do my own work, find my own answers.

So I brought stacks of books into the grove, great volumes of history, science, and, most of all, philosophy. I used these as starting points and began to construct elaborate cosmological models. I built beautiful theories about the origins of space, time, and matter, and the emergence of intelligent life. I discoursed beautifully (I had taken to talking aloud to myself) on the nature of God and the purpose of human life. I proposed theories about the ultimate destiny of the human soul. The professors of theology would have been impressed, no doubt. My logic was airtight, clean, and elegant.

Or so I thought. Just when I would feel the euphoria of having found the answers, of having finally pierced the veil of mystery, a small doubt would creep into my mind. It would be a minor question about one of my more obscure claims. But like a small leak in a dike, the minor doubt would grow into a torrent until my beautiful theories about God and the universe would come crashing down, washing over me in waves of grief and despair.

I would take the scraps and begin again. I would seek out better books by smarter thinkers. I was missing something, always missing something. I wanted a theory of everything, one keystone idea that would hold all other ideas together and keep them from collapsing, but it remained just out of reach. What if the seeds of this keystone idea, the theory that would subsume all theories, were in the next book? The book I had dismissed and tossed aside, or the one I had only skimmed? These thoughts haunted me, and so I poured over the books again, adding several volumes to the list.

Every time I began a new lead, I felt the thrill of pursuit as I chased the final answer, but it always slipped just out of sight, around a corner, or over the horizon. I argued passionately with my doubters, a committee of professors and intellectuals I had formed in my mind, who took issue with nearly every idea I had. This imaginary committee pressed me for evidence, found flaws in my logic, mocked my amateurism, and dismissed my most cherished epiphanies as sophomoric.

I must have been quite a spectacle, pacing back and forth gibbering to myself, arguing angrily with imaginary opponents, and then racing to one of my books to find some key passage to support my argument.

I considered other possibilities, other theories, about the grove. Maybe this had nothing to do with my intellect at all. Maybe this experience was to teach me a lesson in my own limitations, that only God had the answers and I needed to approach him in great meekness.

So I decided to give humility a try. I tossed out my books, found the very center of the grove, and knelt on the ground, something I had not done since being forced to as a child. I clasped my hands together in the way I had seen my mother clasp hers, and in a soft and pleading tone, I acknowledged my nothingness before God's almighty power. I confessed my total and complete dependence on his greatness and glory. I declared that without Him, I was nothing. I confessed I had seen the error of my arrogant ways. I was grateful that Almighty God had given me this opportunity to become humble before him. And if Jesus was part of all this, then I was ready to confess Him as well.

I knelt all day, reminding myself of my nothingness, reminding myself of my newfound humility. With every passing hour I fought feelings of impatience and soothed myself with gentle phrases I had picked up from religious folks, things about God having his own timing and waiting upon the salvation of the Lord.

But how long, really, was I supposed to carry on like this? Just how much praise and admiration did God need until he would finally condescend to my lower-than-dust self? He already held all the cards. He had all the answers. There was no contest between us. He had won. His was always the upper hand. What more did He want from me, if He was even there?

The grove was silent.

I knelt for hours every day, pleading and begging, but all the while becoming angrier, more frustrated. It had seemed that God, or someone, had been seeking me out, and now that I turned in their direction, now that I demonstrated some readiness, I found myself in an empty grove of trees making a fool of myself.

I then realized that each time God had reached out to me I had not been seeking truth. Every time I had contact with God was when I had fallen into some kind of trouble. Seizing this thought, I threatened to cast myself back into Hell where He would have to rescue me all over again—or not; I didn't care anymore. I would go back to Earth and party and get back into the sleaze if that's what he wanted. If that's what it took to get some kind of help, some kind of response. Did He see what He had driven me to? Was He happy now? I would go and get myself into more trouble if that was what it took to get a response.

But my heart couldn't lie. I had no desire for Hell, or Earth, or anything I had been through. I could not have cast myself back into that pit even if I tried. I didn't want Hell. I wanted answers to all my questions. I finally flew into a fit of rage.

"Was all of this some trick?" I screamed into the silence. "Some kind of joke?"

Nothing I tried worked. I had been abandoned. The grove offered me nothing. It held no answers, no heavenly vision, no secret knowledge. I had nowhere to go now. I had lost my standing at the University and detested the thought of returning to Earth as a wandering ghost.

I was frantic, angry, confused. Not since being in Hell had I felt so much uncertainty about my very existence. Nothing made sense to me. Every philosophy and system of belief I had tried came crashing down. Even religion, even worship, gave me the same result: nothing.

The grove was a prison, and there was no way to escape, nowhere to run.

Exhausted and disoriented, I collapsed to the ground and pounded my fist into the earth, trying to feel something. Then I fell into the nothingness of my mind. I could no longer think. I had no will to think. My mind had failed me, and there was nothing I could do about it. When a thought tried to take shape in my mind, it fell apart on contact. There was nothing to hold it, nothing to play with it and shape it into a thousand other thoughts.

Something inside me broke, and I fell into a deep sleep. When I awoke what felt like many days later, I possessed only the power of observation. I could still see, but I had no opinions about what I saw. I could feel, but I had no thoughts about what I felt.

The grove was different somehow, quieter than I had ever noticed, yet humming with life. Birds fluttered in the treetops. Butterflies—were they new or had I only just noticed them?—floated like angels from flower to flower. I observed them for hours in complete fascination.

The stone I lay against was also alive. It breathed; it hummed with its own music. The ground I rested on pulsed with life. By putting my full attention on it, its solidity, I felt a vibration, a music, coming from it. The atmosphere was filled with music for which there is no metaphor, no comparison. It was not a heavenly choir, nor harps, nor any instrument. Everything around me was singing, the stones, the trees, the butterflies, the planets and stars. Everything hummed with a unique frequency that combined with others to make entrancing music that healed and soothed.

As I listened, it seemed as if more life and creation joined the choir. It was not that they began singing, but that my consciousness expanded to absorb them. I had no will to resist anything. No desire to think about what was happening, to weigh it and consider it and ponder its meaning or fit it within some cosmological model. The life around me had no external meaning. The moment was its own meaning; the objects were their own meaning. They were not a means to an end. They did not have a purpose or symbolize something. Their lives were their own end.

I was losing my self and had no desire to struggle. The body, the personality lying in the grove, had been a cage, and now I was set free. But I was not losing my self so much as gaining the millions of selves around me. I was at once becoming nothing and becoming everything.

I became the stones and the soil. I became the grove and began to sing its song. I became the moons and the stars and the galaxies.

For a moment, there was no longer a self to resist this process. At any other time, I might have been frightened, or curious, or excited to tell others. But nothing like that occurred to me. I was swept into a river of Being and was happy to drown in it.

Then it happened. I caught what would later be described to me as my glimpse. Unfolding before me were not planets or stars or galaxies or even life forms. I saw a living, breathing cosmos, pulsating with intelligence, swimming in love, and sustained by grace. It enfolded upon itself in multiple dimensions and layers of time and space. There was no beginning or end, no yesterday and tomorrow. It had no purpose. It was its own purpose. It had no explanation, as it was its own explanation. It was evolving, changing, becoming, creating and destroying, yet always and forever remaining exactly what it was.

And there was no way to think about it, no way to

fit it into a conceptual model. It was not something to be believed in. It was not something to be accepted or rejected as a proposition.

Yet I must have wanted a word, a label. From the depths of my consciousness, I heard a voice coming from a body lying in a grove of trees, that asked, simply, "What am I seeing?"

And then I became that body once again, that self, lying in the grove, and the vision closed as I lay looking at the trees swaying in the nighttime breeze. I lay there for days in a stunned stupor, unwilling to move, basking in the glow of what I had seen, listening to the music of life in my little grove, my little corner of the universe.

I felt—and there is no other word for it—*blessed*. Not because of anything I had done, or thought, or believed, or achieved. I felt blessed just to play a small part in what I saw. To even be a speck of dust in this vast creation was an incomprehensible gift of love. Love was not a feeling; it was the very substance of which all was created.

I refused to move from my place in the grove, refused to stand and walk around, until eventually I became aware of a soft glow at my side, which emanated from a gentle and patient being. He sat next to me, looking at what I was looking at and seeing what I was seeing.

I was not surprised to see him, and the thought of being worthy of his presence never came to mind. The universe I had just glimpsed was not a hierarchy of worthy and unworthy souls. Instead, the infinite creation was God's playground, and we were children learning the rules of play, in the process some hurting, some getting hurt, but everyone learning how to receive an eternity of ever-new joys. I no longer feared this guide who, for some reason, had taken it upon himself to lift me.

"It took so long," I said. "I tried so hard."

"Were you searching for God, or searching for proof of God?" asked my guardian. "What you were looking for was always there; you just had to get out of your own way."

I sat and breathed in this new peace. The grove was holy now.

"Are you ready to move on?" he asked.

"I don't think I ever want to leave this place."

His face was still veiled with light, but the light seemed to smile, and he said, "You never leave completely. The grove stays with you."

I knew he was right. I had to move on. I had to stop running, to stop hiding. We walked to the edge of the trees in silence. I hesitated before reluctantly stepping beyond the trees, not knowing what to expect. I felt myself rising to a new dimension.

15

Entering this new realm was like sitting in a dimly lit room and having someone turn on the lights, all the lights, and realizing then that the room had only been half-lit before. Even though the world of the academies was brighter and freer than any I had lived in, it now seemed drab and gray by comparison. A weight in my chest lifted, a weight I had not before noticed.

An enchanted landscape unfolded before me. I could see great distances with ease, focusing like a telescope, if I wished, on any detail, no matter how far away. Crystalline waterfalls poured into mountain lakes. Animals, only some of which were recognizable from my Earth life, roamed in ancient forests. In structures that looked something like palaces or castles, luminous people went about their business in a relaxed yet earnest way.

But more than any visual delight, the chief joy of this new place was a pervasive feeling of peace and love. I do not mean that everyone was happy or that these emotions were present in myself (though that was also true). Peace and love filled the atmosphere like a substance, a tangible and irresistible energy that penetrated my being.

In this environment, peace did not have to be manufactured as a product of positive thinking or adopting a new life philosophy. Peace *happened* to me; I only had to receive it.

My heart sang in harmony with my surroundings. I felt like I had come home, like I belonged here.

"Is this Heaven?" I asked.

My guardian smiled. "No, not even one of the lower kingdoms. There are realms far beyond this one. This is a place of resting and learning. And of preparation, at least for you."

"Preparation for what?"

"The work. The work of inviting, rescuing, healing. It is the work in which we are all engaged, even you, whether you know it or not."

"I'm in no position to help others," I said. "There have to be people here more qualified for that."

"The work of rescue is specific and individual," he said. "Not just anyone can do it. You must help and be helped by the souls to whom you are bound."

I thought of you, my son, and the old heaviness tightened in my chest. At the University, I had avoided thinking of my earthly ties, apart from the professor, and had liked it that way. Having botched my mortal relationships, and having almost exposed the mother of your child to a gang of body addicts, I wanted to put as much distance as possible between my earthly memories and myself.

"It's not just about your son," said my guardian, knowing my thoughts. "Though he is very much part of it. Most of those who need you left Earth long ago. There is one soul in particular who needs you very much, a soul who mistreated you. He is someone you have deeply hated and despised. You are bound to this soul with cords of pain and hate, and these cords bind both of you. One of you cannot be free without the other, not entirely."

Now it was clear. He spoke of my father who still wandered in that dark underworld I had escaped. I remembered him with a mixture of pity and disgust, not only for his earthly memory, but for that shadowy shell of a man I met in the gutter of the universe.

"I cannot help him," I said. I felt myself sinking, the peace and love slipping away as my heart grew cold. I sickened at the thought of confronting him, but most of all I was terrified at the prospect of going back into Hell. How could I be certain that I would not get sucked in again, that I would not get stuck, like a fly in tar, in that dark and heavy energy?

"I do not have the strength," I confessed.

"None of us have the strength alone. That is why your soul family and all of Heaven are on your side. It will be a process, and it won't be easy, but we will tap into the source of all power."

"You need to find a new man," I said. "One of his brothers, maybe." I also remembered attending the funeral of an aunt, so I knew she must be around here somewhere.

My guardian only laughed. "You have absolutely

nothing to worry about. Worry and anxiety have no place here. God's work is nothing to feel anxious about. You just do your part, that's all."

He spoke with such peace, such stillness, that it was hard to be afraid in his presence.

"I need to know one thing," I said. "Will you be part of it? Will you be part of the rescue mission? I don't have the light to penetrate that darkness. I will go if you can be by my side, but I can't do it without you."

He smiled and said, "You're right. You can't do it without me. I assure you I will be there, but the power and glory is not in me. In your rescue, I was merely a conduit for God's power, an ambassador of the One who sent me, vested with the strength to carry out the job."

He could tell I was skeptical. Was he just being humble about his strength?

He continued, "The point is that it's not about how much glory you have or attain to. It's about the light and glory you are willing to receive. The more you purify your body, the more it becomes a receptacle of powers far beyond anything you could muster of your own will. In Heaven there are no accomplishments to brag about or congratulate yourself for. There are no high achievers. God gives, and you receive or choose not to receive. The choice is always yours.

"Right now, your body is a vehicle of resistance. You and I are still filled with energies that resist God's power and insist on our own will. The more we remove these barriers, the more our bodies become perfect receivers of grace. It's like cleaning the mud from a window so light can pass through uninhibited. This is the real work of rescue, to help one another remove the very barriers we helped one another create. No one sins in a vacuum, and therefore no one repents in a vacuum. Our every action is deeply intertwined with countless other beings and their actions.

"But I'm getting ahead of myself!" he laughed. "You need to settle in and get to know your temporary home."

We arrived at a beautiful building not far from a large temple-like structure that formed the center of this particular community. My guardian told me he had to go and report to his guardian, but that he would return when I was ready.

"I will leave you in the care of a good friend. She will be your guide for a while," he said, then he walked into the temple and disappeared from sight.

I went to the gardens surrounding the temple and sat, pondering the surprising fact that my guardian also had a guardian, for I did not think it possible that more love and wisdom could reside in a person.

I was startled when, to my side, a young woman with dark shoulder-length hair suddenly exclaimed, "You're finally here!" She ran to me and hugged me tightly.

Backing away from her, I said, "I'm sorry, have we met?" At this question, she burst into soulful laughter.

"Yes, we've run into each other a time or two."

And then, holding my face in her hands, she looked deep into my eyes as if to check if anybody was home.

"It looks like you are not fully *here* yet," she said, with only a slight dampening of enthusiasm.

I was a little offended. "What do you mean, not *here*?"

"Not with me, not *here*, not *now*."

I wondered if my guardian had left me with the right person.

"Who are you again?"

In reply, she only hugged me once more. And this time, I hugged her back. It was hard to maintain distance from her, as joy poured from her like a fountain. And she was, next to my guardian, the most beautiful being I had met since my death on Earth.

"Oh, you new arrivals are just so darling," she said.

The shadow of my ego wondered if she was patronizing me. Yet I wasn't offended so much as afraid. I had never seen love and happiness so raw and unrestrained, especially not directed toward me, and I didn't know how to take it. I knew I could never repay her the love she was showing me, and on Earth, love always came with strings attached.

"You still have a lot of resistance in you," she said. "But that's okay. There's so much to learn. I just love this!" Light and love burst from her presence again.

"I'm sorry," I said. "It usually takes me a bit to warm up to people, and where I don't really know you…"

She hugged me again, and then I knew that she was trying to introduce herself to me. On Earth, my habitual defense was to keep a safe distance from people, a distance where they could be managed and assessed for their potential to cause me trouble. This time I allowed some of her light to come into me, and it contained information about who she was. I glimpsed a beautiful soul. Not even my guardian had shared himself with me in this way.

I learned she had died as a mother of young children who were still alive on Earth and for whom she cared deeply. She had been a naturally joyful woman in her life, though had taken on some of the cynicism that comes with the hardness of mortality. Now, unbound by mortal flesh, her beauty and intelligence flowered into a thousand petals of light.

Hugging family and friends freely was a trait she brought from her Earth life. I was tied to her in some way, but could not recall how.

"There is so much to learn," I said. "So much I don't know."

She laughed again. "Time is the one resource we have in abundance. And don't act like it's such a chore. Eternal life is an adventure, not a task to be accomplished. Your path here has been difficult, but this is where the real fun begins."

16

If there ever were a creature committed to enjoyment, I was looking at her. I couldn't resist her infectious happiness and light-heartedness. I relaxed completely in her presence.

"So is that what you do to all new arrivals? Hug them into submission?"

"No," she said matter-of-factly. "Only the ones who really need it."

She touched my shoulder and we found ourselves on a hill overlooking the valley.

"Each of those villages are a kind of receiving place for new arrivals, whether from Earth or from other lower spheres."

"It feels like coming home," I said.

"It might feel like home, but it's not about the place. It's a feeling of awakening and drawing closer to God. God is the safest, most familiar power in the universe, and drawing closer to him always feels like being found, like returning from a long journey."

"Why are there so many different receiving places?" I asked.

"Each one belongs to different soul families, souls bound to one another, helping one another in their journey. But in the end we are all one family. And the experience of no two arrivals is exactly the same. Everyone has unique needs according to their life experiences. After the traumas of life, many souls just need love and rest and healing, a kind of cleansing from Earth's darker energies. Many souls come still wearing their costumes, so they need some time to take them off."

"Costumes?"

"When souls go to Earth, it's as if they enter a grand stage to play a certain role, a certain part, and now that their act is finished and they have left the stage, they need to let go of their costume and reorient to a new life. They adopted their earthly identity, their lines, their script and stage directions so deeply that they carry the momentum of habits and beliefs with them, even though their particular contribution ended. Part of the process of awakening is to view your life from an objective, third-person point of view, to see your life as if from the audience and not as a player on the stage."

The thought of seeing my life again filled me with dread. It was nothing to be proud of, and I wanted to forget it as soon as possible.

Perceiving my thoughts, she said, "Your guardian will take you through the process, and it's wonderful. And I will be there as well, at least for part of it."

I took comfort in knowing she would be there. I

loved feeling her warmth. Though I loved my guardian deeply, his face was still veiled with light, and he seemed untouchable.

"Why can't I see him?" I asked. "Why is he veiled from me? Is it that I'm not at his level?"

"I can see him perfectly," she teased. "He is not keeping himself from you. The veil is over your eyes, not his, because you have set limits on what is possible. Souls cloak themselves with veils of impossibilities. It protects them from the uncomfortable experience of having their perspectives turned upside down. Your veil filters all that you have deemed impossible from your view. As your mind expands and you begin to see your life as infinite opportunity rather than limitation, your discernment will increase. He will appear when you are ready to see him."

Over the next several days she guided me on a tour of this world, teaching me and allowing me to observe the teaching of others. I saw no lecture halls or classes in any traditional sense. Since no two students had the exact same needs, they could not be grouped in cohorts or advanced through pre-designed programs. Learning was driven by the curiosity of the individual, and those who had cultivated their curiosity while on Earth learned quickly and deeply. Asking questions was not just encouraged; it was the primary mode of instruction. There was no curriculum—the individual and his or her desire to learn was the curriculum. A question answered gave rise to more questions, and more questions came from those answers.

My mind was alive with new learning, but it was

not the accumulation of facts and theories. Here, learning was an expansion of the boundaries of the self rather than expansion of one's ego and expertise. All learning was, as my old professor liked to call it, empirical. I did not listen to answers, I experienced them. I wasn't told about the birth of stars or the formation of solar systems; I felt the accumulation of gasses grow denser until witnessing the ignition of nuclear fusion, heat radiating outward, eventually sparking life on coalescing planets. My instructors never asked me to believe in things, never asked me to accept ideas in the abstract or embrace unprovable propositions. Instead, they wanted me to observe them, live them, breathe them.

My teachers spoke of faith, not as the affirmation of beliefs without evidence, but as a kind of patience and courage to move forward, a confidence that things were heading in the right direction, a willingness to step outside the familiar and into the unknown.

I observed the teaching of individuals who had been religious in their life, and in this realm, unlike the theological schools at the University, most of them displayed more openness, more willingness to explore possibilities.

But a few had a hard time assimilating to their new environment. One day as my guide led me to a garden, we passed by a man and his guide talking near a small pond.

"I won't believe it!" said the man, pacing, agitated. "The Bible clearly states it's impossible. Straight is the gate and narrow is the way! I've met people here who were heathens and unbelievers. One of them even cheated me out of some money and wanted to pretend we're all good now. Why did I get thrown in with this lot?"

His patient teacher said, "But with God, all things are possible."

"But the Bible says only those who confess Jesus are worthy of the Kingdom!"

"It also says, *every* tongue shall confess…"

"My preacher warned me about you Universalists. And I won't be deceived by false doctrines, not here, not anywhere. Surely I can't be the only true believer around here. This is *not* what I thought it would be like. I want the real Heaven. I want to talk to a *real* angel." His attending spirit backed away as two other beings appeared, dressed in white, each with beautiful feathered wings, and escorted him into a portal where they disappeared.

"Where did he go?" I asked.

"He's having a bit of transition shock. He'll spend some time in a place that better reflects his expectations, a place where he can enjoy a society of spirits who hold similar beliefs. It appears for now he is still caught up in the idea of 'beliefs.' There's nothing wrong with him. We're all attached in our own ways. He'll open up eventually."

"Angels have wings? I thought that was just in old paintings."

"Well, *his* angels do, at least while escorting him." She paused for a moment, as if tuning in, then smiled. "Yes, that makes sense. In his life, his mother collected angel figurines. He felt protected by them as a small child. Now they will help ease his transition. Rushing the process can shock souls and send them fleeing into lower, more familiar realms, where they share stories about how the 'Shiners' tried to deceive them." She smiled at the word.

"I guess I figured religious folks would have an easier time here," I said.

"Some do. But progress mostly depends on an open heart and mind. Everyone, whether religious or not, must be willing to question cherished beliefs acquired in mortality. No single belief system on Earth held all the truth. Some may have been closer than others, but confusion and human weakness tainted all of them in some way.

"Those who advance more easily view their religion as a vehicle rather than a destination. But many spirits arrive expecting to see their beliefs play out exactly as they imagined on Earth. I've seen many souls lecturing their guides about how things ought to be. "

"Well, I wasn't religious, so maybe that puts me at an advantage in learning stuff," I said.

"Not so fast," she said. "Everyone arrives with beliefs that potentially slow progress. Some, for example, hold onto beliefs about their own unworthiness of God's love."

With a gentle wave of her hand, a memory flashed in my mind of me prying myself from the loving embrace of my angelic rescuers, falling back into lower spheres.

"Yeah, good point," I said. "School of hard knocks. I caused myself a lot of unnecessary trouble."

"But it *was* necessary. It was necessary because it

happened. All that happens, all manifest phenomena, is for our experience and growth. But not all lessons are hard. Today we're going to play."

She led me to a garden on the outskirts of our village. Tall, prehistoric trees lined a kind of meadow, and stone pathways meandered through flower beds and shrubs. Flowers in colors I never knew existed shone in the light. Each plant was alive and had a kind of personality. Each one seemed happy to exist.

She did not lecture me about the flowers' names, genus, or species, but introduced me to them as she would to friends. She took me to a flowering bush and told me to sit by it and still my mind.

"What do you see?" she asked, gesturing to the bush.

"Beautiful flowers," I answered.

"Then all you are seeing is a label, a mental symbol that separates you from the thing itself. Stay with them in patience and you will see the flowers only when you no longer see 'flowers.' You will see them when they stop being a 'thing.' True learning, as true love, is the process of closing the gap between the self and the other."

For a long while, as she tended to other plants in the garden, I sat and thought about the flowers, their beauty, studying their patterns and colors, searching for some way to better comprehend them. I tried expressing my appreciation for them in my heart. I tried to deepen my admiration for them, all the while monitoring whether or not it was "working."

"You are smothering them with yourself," she said from a distance, not looking up from her work. "You are making this about you. You want something from them, something beautiful and illuminating, so you are grasping at them. You must receive them, not try to flatter them with your own enlightenment." She was right. Mentally, I was crawling all over the flowers, looking for an entrance. I relaxed and quieted my mind, but my thoughts were scattered. Was I doing it wrong? Should I try a different plant? I also wondered secretly if this was a pointless waste of time. Perhaps we could just move on to a new topic.

She knew my thoughts were a restless mess and cheerfully told me not to worry so much. "I'll give you a little nudge," she said. She gently placed her hand at the bottom of my back and moved it upward, over my neck, then over the top of my head until her hand covered my eyes. Then with her other hand, she touched the plant.

I felt the pure joy, the ecstasy of my consciousness leaving the confines of my own body. I don't know if I entered the flower, if the flower entered me, or if there was even any useful difference between the two of us. I felt the happiness of the flower, its joy for simply being. It wanted to play, expressing an openness to cooperate with my will regarding its role in the garden. If I wanted, I could have helped it grow in some other way, some other direction. I say helped, but in fact its roots were my feet, and its branches were my arms. I only had to move them. But I didn't want to change it. Simply being with it was enough.

She lifted her hand from my eyes and, with a sense of loss, my consciousness slowly withdrew from the intelligence I had labeled a flower. Now I didn't know what it was; it was pure mystery, transcending language, yet it was now the most familiar, most intimate thing I had experienced.

"At its best," she said, "creation is not the manipulation of matter and energy. Our gardeners do not cut and prune—such violence would be unthinkable here. They dance with the spirits of these amazing beings. It's our privilege to participate in the ongoing creations of God.

"As a recent arrival, your consciousness is still object-oriented. True growth comes from the ability to view other things not as objects but as extensions of the self. You have glimpsed the life of a flower. Just imagine what it is to glimpse the life of other human souls—first those closest to you, then extending outward."

So that's what this was about. I had tried to put my father and the impending rescue mission out of my mind, not wanting it to spoil my fun. But here he was again.

"I'm not ready," I said. "I still have so much more to learn."

I knew this was selfish of me. Here I was, playing and learning in this paradise, while he endured horrors my mind could no longer imagine. I felt real pity for him, genuine compassion, but I did not trust myself to lead the mission.

"You need to do this work while your consciousness is still somewhat earthbound, before you get too distracted playing with your newfound powers in this sphere. Spiritual progress can actually be difficult in this realm. Many spirits get stuck at this level, believing it to be Heaven.

"We can play in God's creation with eyes wide open, fully awake, or we can play in dreams—dreams that, as you have discovered, can quickly turn to nightmares. Even in the lower dimensions of Heaven, which you have not yet glimpsed, certain desires will eventually run their course, at which point a soul will seek to draw closer to the Source of all reality again. Until we come to know ourselves fully, as God knows us, until we view reality with the mind of God, our work and play will carry a hint of dissatisfaction.

"In this world, you have some order and direction to help you, but as you have seen, there are many worlds to draw away your attention, and the risk of becoming lost again is real. You have your agency, and we cannot force you to do the work, but if you run away, your progress will stall, and there's no telling how long before you find your way back."

"Why *my* progress?" I said. "I thought this was about my father in Hell."

"You still see yourself as fundamentally separate from him. That is exactly the point of this work, to destroy that delusion. Trust in the process. He needs you. You need each other. It will begin tomorrow, if you choose."

She reached out and gently touched my shoulder again. This time I found myself alone on an elegantly carved stone balcony, which I understood was part of my living quarters. I lingered there and took in the expansive landscape before me. It was evening, and the sun seemed to set very slowly, as if lingering to more fully grace the mountains with golden light.

Everything here was on a larger scale than I had ever experienced on Earth. The forests extended from the rolling foothills to the shores of an enormous lake. Dotting the forests and meadows, I could see the spires of what looked like temples or castles, each surrounded by cottages and houses one could only dream of in a fairy tale. I thought of what a pleasure it would be to get lost in these forests that were so full of life and color. There was so much to see, so much to discover.

I was tempted in that moment to run, to flee whatever "work" my friends had prepared me for. They were concerned about my progress, but I felt like I could spend an eternity in this place and be just fine. And as for my father, they could easily find better, more qualified souls to oversee his rescue. I wished the best for him; I had let go of my old hard feelings, since my Earth life seemed so distant now.

But I also knew every time I ran from their invitations in the past, every time I let the fear of the unknown dictate my decisions, things soured quickly. So I resolved to carry on, to follow through with the process they had planned.

As a gentle darkness came over the land, the vibrations I had perceived as music slowed to a restful hum. The landscape and its inhabitants moved in harmony with the natural rhythms of activity and stillness, work and rest. And now the landscape slowed to a restful state.

Night came, but nothing like total darkness. I don't know if they were closer or if my powers of perception had increased, but the sky became a colorful garden of stars and galaxies and planets. In my youth, when I still believed in an afterlife, I had imagined it as a foggy realm of ghost-like beings floating in clouds with angels. The afterlife of my youth was a vague and dreamlike place, nothing like what I now experienced. Here I was more alive and awake than I had ever felt on Earth. I was surrounded by real people, real animals, real life, living on an actual planet. Although I was in a different universe than before, it was still a real universe, made of real matter and energy.

I recalled my time in the abyss of Hell, and as a ghost on the Earth, with a kind of disgust. Even the University, which had been such a place of rest and relief, felt distant and insignificant. My life in each of those places on my journey was dreamlike compared to the vividness of this new realm. The temptation to view this reality as my permanent home was only tempered by my experiences of awakening into clearer, more vibrant levels of life.

I knew there must be more to the cosmic drama than eternal leisure or the satisfaction of curiosity. I became more resolved to follow the guidance of my friends. My real education was about to begin.

17

Rest in this world was nothing like sleep on Earth. It was a deep and dreamless sleep, but also a conscious sleep. My whole body and soul melted into the stillness of night. When morning came, it felt like a rebirth, as if the whole world was also reborn and awaiting new acts of creation. Nothing here was monotonous, no mass production, no daily grind.

I was ready for whatever awaited, but still apprehensive. My guardian met me, and sensing my nervousness, filled me with love. He told me I was not alone in this, and that I would be supported by unseen friends and ancestors.

At the center of this community, like the others throughout the landscape, stood a large temple-like structure that formed the focal point of activity. Large crystal spires lined the exterior, while inside tall columns supported the ceilings. The architecture was simple and elegant without being too showy or too ornate. This would be the place of my training as well as the point of entry for rescuing my father.

Inside, we entered a large, dark room where the only light was what emanated from my guardian. I felt safe in his presence and knew that as long as he was with me I could make this journey.

"Your preparation begins with understanding who you are and what you are doing," he said. "I will teach by analogy. Until you are capable of direct perception, analogies—while they have their limits—will suffice.

"We are all part of a vast and beautiful work of art. Wholeness comes with working in harmony with God's creative processes. When you resist, the result is confusion and discord, a sense of enmity with creation.

"To exist in a state of competition and comparison, to assert one's glory over another, or to see yourself in a game of trying to win God's approval is to exist in a state of self-delusion. Freedom comes from directly perceiving your divine nature, not just learning about it intellectually. And there is only one divine nature. God is one.

"The universe is not a hierarchy of the righteous and the wicked or the intelligent and the ignorant. There is only one kind of being in the universe, and all creation comes from that Being and is fundamentally good. Beings who know they are part of God are sometimes labeled as righteous; beings who have forgotten are sometimes labeled as evil. But the difference is one of accurate perception versus ignorance, not essential nature.

"Evil is not an inherent quality of any being's soul, but a temporary condition of ignorance. God's work is not to sort out the good from the bad or the righteous from the wicked, but to awaken souls to an understanding of their true selves. Once souls understand this fully, they will return to the God who gave them life.

"This is our work and God's work—not to sort and judge, but to awaken to eternal life, or more accurately, to *return* to eternal life."

My guardian pointed to an empty space before us, where a large, ornate vase appeared. He must have pulled it from my own mind, for it was similar to one I had seen in a museum during mortality and had paused to admire longer than the rest. But this version was much taller, at least twice my height.

Unlike the one from my memory, this vase was not a dead piece of ceramic, but vibrated with life and intelligence. It was a conscious intelligence, but it did not comprehend itself. It did not understand itself as something beautiful because it had not experienced anything other than itself.

Suddenly a crack formed at the base and traveled up the side, and I felt a keen sense of loss as the fissure split the vase in two pieces, each piece falling to the floor. Now each half of the vase saw the other half, and the vase began to comprehend itself. The halves regarded one another with fascination and fear. Each half coveted the other's beauty but also hated the other's brokenness as it hated its own brokenness.

More cracks formed in the halves, which then split into more pieces. Now with more pieces, the competition grew fiercer and the fragmentation continued, fragments breaking into fragments that broke into more fragments. Soon I saw millions of pieces of painted ceramic in combat, cutting and getting cut, breaking and being broken, each one fighting for its own legitimacy, its own worth.

Then a fragment appeared that had a perfect memory of the vase's wholeness. It contained the master plan, the whole image of the lost vase. It knew how to mend the brokenness. Though the work seemed impossible, this shard bound itself to one fragment, then another, and then another. The vase began to mend, but the work was slow, as thousands of fragments filled the room in a swirling cloud. Many shards only decided to come together after they had exhausted all other options for finding a sense of completeness. I watched in wonder and delight as hundreds of pieces forgot their self-importance and found their place in the whole.

The work was not random. Two pieces could not come together in just any order. For the art to be perfectly restored, each broken piece had to seek out the others to which it had been bound and mend itself with those pieces, no matter how long it took. Some pieces came together easily and naturally. Other pieces tried to come together but kept jabbing and crashing into one another awkwardly, binding themselves in all the wrong ways. These pieces yearned for wholeness but still insisted on their own brokenness. Only by giving up their identity as broken fragments could they find their fit, their harmony.

Sometimes several other pieces, which had already bound themselves to others, had to wait until two pieces found their fit before they could come into place. Like a complex jigsaw puzzle, when a key piece had found its place, it set off a chain reaction, enabling other pieces of the puzzle to fall into place.

So the binding and mending happened one fragment at a time. At first the work seemed absurdly slow and impossible, but there was momentum in it, for as the vase began to form, other fragments caught the vision and began to search for their place.

Eventually the work completed, and the vase was different, even more beautiful than before, with tiny fracture lines, like scars, giving it an aged and weathered appearance. It now seemed even more alive than before. Having experienced fragmentation, the vase comprehended its wholeness. Having experienced its own death, it comprehended its life. Having experienced its own destruction, it now comprehended itself as creation and beauty.

"The old life," my guardian said, "is largely defined by a sense of fragmentation and separation—separation from God and separation from one another. We only experienced *ourselves* as real and found it impossible to truly see into the life of another soul. We experienced ourselves as fragments, and we tried to make ourselves whole by filling ourselves with more of our self, asserting our own greatness, which caused only more fragmentation.

"We thought of ourselves as individuals, and as an individual, the natural thing was to compare yourself with others, to see how you measured up, to see where you fit in the great game of losers and winners. Who was the smartest, the prettiest, the strongest, and the richest? It even infected spiritual life—who was the most righteous, the most enlightened, the wisest, the most loving? The journey to Hell is this striving to win in a supposedly hostile universe, competing against other souls who are also striving to make themselves great.

"Awakening means releasing your individual claim to greatness and glory and finding your place in the fabric of creation. This requires seeing other fragmented beings as essential, not as hostile, to our quest for wholeness.

"You have come a long way. But escaping Hell was not about leaving a certain space. In a sense, you are not returning to Hell to rescue your father. You are still there with him, still bound to him in all the wrong ways.

"Only mending and binding your hearts according to God's plan will make things right. Generations of ancestors await your reconciliation. It will cause a chain reaction that will work backward through your soul family as they are released from their contribution to your brokenness. Your change of heart will free you, and it will also free them to continue their journeys."

I still didn't understand what my extended family had to do with this. In mortal life, I had little connection with them, and I had no real interest in my ancestors.

"Why can't my soul family just go about their own business, growing at their own pace?" I said. "How could my father and I be holding them back?"

"Think of your soul family as a body. In the old life, if you were to smash your foot, the rest of the body could not indifferently go about its business. The whole body feels the pain, and the whole body must attend to healing. But we must extend this analogy to understand what is really happening in the human family. The broken foot and its consequent pain cannot be blamed on the foot alone. The entire body, all of its systems, played a part in that act, and therefore, all of the systems are responsible for it.

"You cannot imagine the hands or nose congratulating themselves for their own righteousness while the foot suffers. A body divided against itself in that way could not live. A healthy body experiences pain as a whole and joy as a whole. When one part of the body is released from pain, the entire body rejoices.

"Your soul family, extending back to your distant ancestors, is inextricably tied to your life on Earth. They provided the genetic material for your body as well as the cultural environment in which you lived and breathed. So much of the challenges and inclinations, good and bad, that you believed were uniquely yours were actually a shared burden—shared with them.

"Instead of viewing yourself as you truly were, a good soul heroically advancing the spiritual evolution of the human family, you saw yourself as a lone individual losing at a game in which the rules were stacked against you."

In the space where the vase had been, there appeared the image of a human body. I was unsettled to see that it was a model of my image, my body, on display before me. But I did not perceive it in the normal way. My eyes were opened so that I was able to see every part of it, every tissue, every cell, and every system.

Yet there were no parts. I did not just perceive the physicality of cells and tissues and nerves. I saw their origin, their life cycle, their function, and the way they formed the whole. These were not parts working together like a machine. They were a single, indivisible unit. The body was perfect and healthy. But, like the vase, it did not perceive itself as such.

I perceived the body at a microscopic level, and watched as a virus infected a cell, then another cell, and spread throughout the entire body. The infection was fierce, permeating every tissue. The body grew pale as its various systems shut down until it was on the brink of death. Then a cell infused with light started its own kind of infection, an infection of health and energy that spread from cell to cell. Each cell learned how to overcome the virus and flourish again. The body returned to full health, but now, because it had experienced the opposition of infection, it enjoyed itself as alive and healthy. It was no longer susceptible to the virus, as it was inoculated against its effects. Joy and appreciation only came through overcoming opposition.

As the body returned to life, my guardian said, "Witness the resurrection of Christ."

I was startled at this and worried that he had blasphemed, as this was clearly *my* body we were looking at.

He heard my thoughts and smiled at my concern. "This is Christ consciousness coming alive in you, as it must come alive in all, giving new life to all humanity."

The body disappeared, and we stood alone in the

darkness, as I tried to absorb my teaching. He said, "Analogies help, but their symbolic nature still creates distance between your mind and the thing itself. Awakening is the process of dissolving barriers between yourself and pure reality."

"I still don't understand what all this is about," I said, "all this talk of awakening and growing. I have been saved from Hell and am now in Heaven. If you need my help getting my dad here, I am fine to do that. But isn't that the important thing? Haven't I been, as they used to say on Earth, *saved*?"

I felt a kind of joyful mirth coming from my guardian, almost laughter, not patronizing or mocking, but a kind of delight in my question.

"In the end, the only thing to be saved from is ignorance and our incorrect perception of reality. Salvation is the process of removing the veil of ignorance from our mind. To see something purely and understand it purely is to love it purely. As our consciousness expands beyond the boundaries of the self, as we assimilate each new life into our being, or rather, as our life extends into creation, our joy expands until, eventually, we share in the mind of God.

"Righteousness and sin are not about obeying or disobeying a list of commandments. Righteousness is anything that deepens our powers of accurate perception or, in other words, love. Sin is anything that obscures or distorts our capacity to love. Whenever we resist or deny reality, we thicken the veil of darkness surrounding our minds, which keeps us from seeing and therefore loving. Heaven is not Heaven because of beautiful scenery. It is Heaven simply because it is the dwelling place of beings who are no longer fettered by veils of self-delusion.

"Hell is the exact opposite. In Hell, your mind was so darkened by confusion that we needed to create an opening, just one moment of clarity and love. It had to be a moment in your life—the birth of your son—when your awareness was least polluted by self-concern. You were touched by grace because grace is the gift of sight, of seeing things as they really are, not through the lens distorted by our pride, appetites, opinions, and judgements. True sight leads inevitably to true love.

"Which brings us to the next stage of your growth. It will be among the most painful and joyful experiences you have had yet. You must open the book of your life and review its wisdom and secrets."

I had feared this moment. I felt the familiar desire to run.

18

You, my son, know as well as anyone why I would shrink in fear at the prospect of seeing my life again. I was not a good person on Earth. I hurt people. I caused pain. I lived in pain and spent most of my time numbing that pain with drugs and alcohol. I coped by running, always running, and cutting off most of my relationships, one by one, until I was alone, striving for money and recognition in my career, the only things I had left.

I did not fear the review because of shame. My guardian was incapable of shaming me. But I resisted facing my life in his presence because I knew there would be no room for self-justifying excuses. In the light of such a presence, there was no possibility for self-deception.

"Can't I just acknowledge my sinfulness before God and ask forgiveness?" I asked.

"God is not interested in your apology; God is interested in your transformation," he said. "And transformation only happens in the light of full awareness of truth. That awareness must begin with confronting the truth of your own life exactly as it was. You, as most all human beings, lived in a dreamlike state of self-delusion, so busy managing your image and self-importance that you rarely lived in reality."

"Isn't there another way?" I said. "Why should I have to get dragged through it all again? That doesn't seem like progress. Isn't progress about moving on and letting go of the past, not looking backward?"

"You are right," he said. "That is why you will not be *reliving* any part of your life. You will see it in full awareness for the first time. The moments of your life that you truly lived, the moments of full consciousness, even painful or dark moments, do not need to be reviewed. The moments in which you reflected honestly on the reality of a situation without defensiveness and self-justifying stories will not be part of the review."

This did little to comfort me. Such times of clarity would be few and far between. If my book of life recorded moments of self-delusion, my book must look like the collected works of Shakespeare.

"Well, we'd better get started if we want to finish in a reasonable time," I said bravely.

He smiled and said, "You are afraid."

"No, I'm not. If this is what we have to do, let's do it and get it over with." I was hardening myself for the experience, digging in, bracing for the storm.

"You are not fearful?" he asked. And I knew I was busted. He held his hand near my chest and pulled a thin string of brownish light from my body. Still attached to me, it sort of danced in the space between his hand and my body. It was a thread of fear, almost as if it were alive and had an existence of its own. And it wasn't just any fear. It was the fear of this very moment, this situation, the fear of seeing my life.

"This is your newest fear," he said. "You just created it, but that isn't the problem. You kept it alive by denying its existence. You did not experience it in full awareness, in full honesty, so it hid in your body until it could speak its truth. Let's give it another chance."

I studied the brown light with fascination.

"Are you afraid?" he asked again.

"Yes," I said, and I felt the truth of it. Emotion welled up in me, and I felt tears coming, but again my instincts kicked in, and I held back. It would be humiliating to cry like a little child.

"Who are you trying to impress by pretending to be strong?"

"I don't know," I said. "You. Maybe God."

"You are not doing God or anyone any favors by denying reality. The denial of reality is the source of all sin. If you are afraid right now, do not deny yourself that reality. Look into it. See what's there."

I looked into the brown light still dancing before me. When I looked at it, my gaze became the focused light of a movie projector, shining through a film and projecting the recent moment in the space before us. The fear took shape as an image, and I saw myself standing next to my guardian just moments before, talking with him about how it was time to review my life. The picture was three-dimensional and perfectly comprehensible. My consciousness merged with the image, and I fully felt the fear. It was not so much that I chose to feel it; there was simply no denying it. The fear possessed a kind of beauty and purity. The fear was truth, and there was no shame in it.

In a flash of light, the scene disappeared, sending a shockwave of energy outward from our presence into our surroundings, into the planet, into the universe, and into God. It was as if I had not only denied myself that reality, I had denied it to God, who now felt my fear just as I had felt it.

Joy poured from my guardian's presence, like the joy of a parent seeing a child take its first step. I felt lighter and happier, as if a small weight had been lifted, a weight I didn't know I was carrying. A thread of light still danced before me, but now it was shimmering brightly. It was still the experience of the fear, but it was no longer a burden. It had been transformed into a delight.

But it was still attached to other threads of energy now rising up, like a thick cord of multicolored yarn attached to the fabric of my body.

"That fear, that experience, did not happen in a vacuum. It was not created out of nothing. It was intertwined with other experiences, which are entangled with still other experiences. Are you ready to have a closer look?"

My apprehension disappeared. Liberating that small piece of energy emboldened me, and I wanted to see where it led. He held his hand in front of my chest and drew out multicolored strings of light, each filled with life and intelligence. My body was the book of life, and it poured forth a confession in an explosion of images from my past.

Events from my life, beginning at my death, unfolded before me. I saw the car wreck that ended my life, the horror that set me fleeing, running as I always had from the consequences of my choices. But now the full weight of that action was before me in exquisite detail, the pure, undeniable truth of the wreck I had caused. I saw my body in the torn steel, smelling of whiskey and blood.

Then the horror I had tried to deny for so long. From the back seat of the other car came the whimpering cries of a child, "I'm cold. Mom, I'm cold." Cold, but alive! And another child? His pale face moved to the side and spit blood onto the seat. Hurt, but yes, alive. But the mother, I could hardly see her in the mangled heap. She tried, instinctively, to reach back. Was it to touch, to comfort? But her hand fell short. The steering wheel, pinned against her chest, stopped her heart as her lungs filled. Bits of glass glistened in her moonlit hair. Her muscles relaxed, and her body grew still.

Here was a truth too great to bear. Ever since my death, I had tried to deny this possibility. I tried to convince myself, when I thought of the wreck at all, that I was the only casualty of my stupidity. But denial was now a luxury I could not indulge.

I saw the children, weeks later, sitting in their classrooms, staring out the classroom window at nothing in particular, falling behind in their work, the topic of hushed conversations among teachers. I saw visits to a cemetery. A crayon drawing and hand written notes stuck to a rain-soaked gravestone. Then the quiet evenings, meals where the only sound was the hum of the refrigerator and the clinking of forks on plates. The children's father tried to engage them.

"What are you up to?"

"Nothing."

"How is school going?"

"Fine."

Then he'd lay awake. When he slept, he forgot, but in the early hours he would awaken to the memory, the knock at the door, the police officer, hat in hand. *The children are fine, but I'm sorry your wife didn't...*

Their grief, their pain, crashed upon me in waves. I wanted to hide under a mountain. I longed for the extinction of my soul and begged my guardian to stop the scene. I knew I made many mistakes in my life, but never imagined anything like this. I had killed an innocent person. She lost her life not for any choice of her own, but because of my selfishness.

I could not bear this; the burden was too great, too heavy. The paradise of this realm now became a Hell, a prison. I did not belong here. I did not deserve a fraction of the kindness and goodness that had been shown me here. I could never rescue my father. I belonged with him in Hell, forever.

With these thoughts the scene of the car wreck closed around me, condensed into their tiny threads and entered again into my body. They wrapped me like heavy chains, and I was determined to carry them forever.

"Are you choosing to keep this?" said my guardian. "You could give it to God."

"It can't be that easy," I said. "That's just too easy. Give it to Christ, to God, and suddenly it's all better. Everything is all better, all fixed, and everyone is happy. None of that makes what I did okay. None of that changes the consequences."

My guardian did not speak. I could tell he was also in pain. We stood for a while in silence. Then my guardian spoke in his wise and loving voice.

"A part of God is in you. If you deny yourself the full force of the reality of your life, then you are denying the divine part of you. God is pure reality, and for you to deny or run from any part of reality, especially the reality of your own existence, is to deny God. True repentance is not sprinkling sugar on top of hard experience or pretending everything is fine. Repentance is facing truth in all of its wonderful and gritty detail. Your consciousness cannot comprehend it now, but someday you will see there is beauty and redemption in even the ugliest things. Even the worst life can become a work of art, depending on whether you choose to face it or run from it."

He put his hand on my shoulder, and I felt his healing love.

"By sharing your pain with God, you are not denying it or trying to escape its consequences. Cleansing it from your body is the only way to truly face it. But by taking all of this into yourself and keeping it, you are making the single greatest human error. You are viewing yourself as an isolated individual fighting and losing in the battle of life instead of as an interconnected being woven into the fabric of creation."

We stood in the darkness of the temple room. My guardian knew I needed to rest. The silence was soft and nurturing, healing even.

"When you are ready, I invite you to explore the experience again without fear. See where it goes."

There, in the darkness of the temple, I debated whether to run, to leave my guardian forever and seek refuge in one of the lower realms. I could return to the grove and reverse this whole process. Perhaps I could return to Earth and numb myself with the flesh addicts. But the thought sickened me. What was I running from? The experience had once again embedded itself in my body. Wherever I ran, there it would be, with me still. There was nowhere to run. I could not live in the lower realms knowing what I knew now.

There was no suicide here. No way to extinguish the fact of one's existence. I knew that no matter where I went or what I chose, it would only be a change of scenery, not a change of being. I did not deserve healing or grace, but that was not really the choice. The choice was not about receiving a free pass from God and escaping consequence; it was a choice of facing truth or fleeing from it, of taking reality as it was or denying it. Once I chose to embrace the full, unvarnished, undiluted truth, I would share it with God, and a burden shared with God is the best kind to bear. Truth is grace. Reality is grace.

The sudden clarity of the thoughts streaming into my mind surprised me. I wasn't sure if these thoughts were my own or were being given to me, but it didn't matter. I was learning that it didn't matter. Truth was truth, and it did not originate in any individual's mind.

In this world, no one could take credit for new insight.

This time, I did not need my guardian to prod me. By an act of will, I pulled the memory from my body again, and hundreds of living images related to the wreck appeared. Each image was a starting place, an entry point into a vast network of interrelated events. The crash was the focal point of a web of people and choices that it had affected.

19

I entered the wrecked car and heard cries and felt the physical pain of the children. Again, guilt and unworthiness crushed me, and I pulled back from the scene.

"Do not make this about your own feelings," counseled my guardian. "Repentance is not about you. Enter into the experience; see the others in all truth and love them."

I relaxed my body and entered the scene again. This time I did not hear the cries of the children as the voices of my condemnation, but I heard them with the love and compassion of their mother. I wanted to comfort them, to hold them, to tell them it would be all right and that help was on the way. In that moment, they were my children, too.

The scene then exploded into various images from their life after the collision, the love they felt from their father, the way they came together as a family and loved one another through the tragedy. I experienced their grief exactly as it was. God was not punishing me with their grief and the reality of their pain and their disrupted life. As long as the review was about their pain and not *my reaction* to their pain, the scene was a sacred window into their souls. But when the scene became a story of my irredeemable guilt, it contracted and lost the touch of grace.

Once I had experienced a particular thread of the web in its fullest, the scene would change, go back to the focal point and begin again.

The bottle of booze spilled on the floor of my smashed car, amazingly still unbroken, but the smell of whiskey hung thick in the air. Information poured from the bottle, telling its story—the money exchanged at the store, the distributors, the distilleries, the grain in the fields, the farmers, the sun and rain nourishing the grain, the grain sprouting from the soil. Everything had a story to tell.

But the alcohol in the blood of my lifeless body told a different story. It contained my choice to drink hard that night and mingle alcohol with prescription painkillers. I saw my choice to ignore a voice, a voice I discerned even in my drunkenness, that warned me against getting into the car. A coworker watched me, almost stopped me, almost offered me a ride, but didn't want to embarrass me, didn't want the hassle.

I followed the colorful, interwoven threads of light. Choices connected to other choices. Every drink I had taken in my past came into view. I saw my descent into alcoholism, which was connected to my party years in college, but the other threads of choice were not entirely my own. My decisions were intertwined with the choices of others.

One thread of images led, like a branching tree, to my father's overdrinking. I saw his heavy drinking and how he indifferently let booze lie around the house, within reach of a curious and mischief-seeking twelve-year-old boy. The threaded images of his drinking became more abundant when they connected to the years following the war, and these in turn were connected to his own father's problem with alcohol, which, while not as heavy, still burdened his family.

The scenes did not unfold as separate events, but as a play of interrelated moments that transcended time and normal perceptions of cause and effect. The events affected one another across time and space. None of the actions I viewed occurred in isolation, but were bound together in a web; movement in one place sent trembling vibrations to the whole.

Once fully understood, the threads of alcoholism faded away, and my awareness returned to the scene. I now saw the woman who had been driving the car. Moments from her life exploded before my mind. She laughed a lot as a child, and liked to jumpscare her friends. She married at 19 and started a family young. She wished, later in life, she had traveled or gone to college, but she also loved motherhood and made a point of letting her kids get as dirty as they wanted playing outside. People liked being around her without fully understanding why.

She was not perfect, but she was honest about her imperfection. If she were jealous or annoyed, she would say so. Some could not bear this honesty, interpreting it as overconfidence or indifference.

Strangely, I loved her. Not in any romantic or sentimental way, but I simply delighted in her life, her person. Was she really this remarkable, or was I perceiving her this way because I was privy to this multidimensional view of her person? Maybe every soul, known deeply, intimately, becomes captivating to us.

In glimpsing her life, I understood the arbitrariness of human fame and praise and recognition. In mortality, this woman would have been considered one of the unsung masses. She was not well-educated. Physically, she was not homely, but not strikingly attractive, either. She was not accomplished at any one particular talent. Yet her life seemed no less radiant, no less important than that of a famous saint. My habit of putting people into categories of greatness, importance, and accomplishment was entirely destroyed.

I perceived that there were no famous people in Heaven. To think in terms of fame and greatness was a habit of the ego-bound human mind. God had no use for the concept of historical greatness.

When I suddenly realized I had robbed the Earth of such a bright soul, it seemed to me an unforgivable crime, no matter how much grace or mercy was available. But again, when my thoughts directed inward and focused on my own guilt, when I made her life about me and my mistake, the un-lived images merged back into my body to hide. Only when I forgot myself did the scenes live out their life for my full comprehension. The more I delighted in the beauty of her life, the more her life blessed me with its grace.

As the scenes played out, I knew that I knew her.

She was familiar, friendly. Or was it simply that I wanted to know her? As my mind pondered this question, certain scenes now played before me as if to provide an answer. I saw her buckling her children into their car seats after picking them up from her mother's home earlier that night.

As I saw this, I also saw myself in the same moments as I left the party, dazed and stumbling, fumbling with my keys.

I wanted with all my soul to stop the events from playing out, but they had already happened. I was viewing a reality that could not be altered. The time for making choices, at least regarding this, had passed. She drove through the darkness, the kids dozing in the back seat, rocked to sleep by the gentle back-and-forth sway of the car as it made its way through the canyon highway.

I saw her thoughts as she reflected on the day's events and planned the mundane chores she needed to do the next day. Her youngest son's birthday was coming up, and she hadn't yet thought about what to get him. She had bills to mail but needed more stamps, and she made a mental note to pick some up at the grocery store the following morning. The car also needed gas, but that could wait until a paycheck came in a few days. Beneath that thought was a subtle resentment that her husband had recently passed up a higher-paying but more stressful job. What about the stress of rationing gas and groceries?

Amid these thoughts she was overcome with an ominous feeling and looked into the back to make sure the kids were buckled in. She checked her speed and slowed to the speed limit. There had been deer on the road, and her senses heightened. When she leaned forward into a position of greater alertness, she noticed the full moon, how it lit the hillsides and made the road visible even beyond her headlights. She breathed deeply and relaxed. No music played. After a busy day, she welcomed the stillness of the car. She breathed again, satisfied that life was good.

Miles away, I left the party in a foul mood. One of my coworkers, a guy I believed was gunning for a promotion that was rightfully mine, had been making a complete fool of himself, cracking jokes and inserting himself into conversations. The problem was that others did not see it that way. They laughed and said "Tell that story about the time..." He was the life of the party. Couldn't they see the way he sucked up, how he worked the room like a politician? Such were my petty thoughts. The game wasn't going my way and I had to get out of there as fast as I could, running away again.

A cloud of light surrounded me, trying to penetrate my dark thoughts with the message to slow down, to stop, to think. But my mind was muddied with a thick veil of hatred and drunkenness. There was no opening in my spirit, no softness, no place to receive anything.

That faker, that backslapping good ol' boy would get the job, and I'd be overlooked again. I drove fast, and the speed felt good, dangerous. It was almost as if I *wanted* something to happen. I had no intention of getting in a crash that would hurt others. But it was as if I dared fate to do something to me.

Further up the canyon, the woman breathed again and loosened her grip on the steering wheel. The foreboding feeling had given way to a sense of peace, a sense of blessedness. I saw light gathering around her and the children, but no message of intervention came; it was a kind of embrace. Her angels were embracing her because this was her language. I was shown that throughout her life she had the peculiar habit of giving people, sometimes mere acquaintances, warm and joyful hugs. In this way her angels and guardians were speaking to her.

My car picked up speed around curves, careening recklessly from side to side. When the opportunity for me to make a different decision was reduced to zero, I crossed the centerline, and her car appeared around the bend. My speed was too great, my reaction too slow.

A loud explosion rang out upon impact. The driver's side of both vehicles took the greatest hit. I was killed instantly, and she died only a few moments later. It was a miracle the children made it with as few injuries as they had.

My spirit lingered near the wreck for a moment, turned from the beckoning light and ran to find cover in the mass of tangled darkness below. I watched as my spirit voluntarily descended into Hell, coaxed and prodded by those hideous beings—my father among them—who had nurtured my demise.

But my consciousness did not follow that thread. Instead I followed the wonderful soul who had now departed mortality because of me. I saw her enter a higher realm, welcomed with warm embraces from beings too lovely for words. Then I only saw scenes of her afterlife that touched mine.

She struggled to forgive me for cutting her life short, for robbing her of the chance to raise her children. At first she took some satisfaction in knowing I had not survived the wreck and that I had descended into the darkness. Later, when the time for my deliverance had come, my guardian approached her and invited her to be part of the mission to rescue me from Hell. But she refused, believing I had not yet paid enough.

When my guardian showed her my life, her heart softened. She saw me. She knew I was not paying for something in Hell. I was not satisfying a debt to justice, but was simply suffering, a fellow soul whom she had the power to help. She knew it was within her power to offer peace, and to withhold that offering would bind us together in pain. So she joined the mission to snatch me out of Hell and stood by my guardian during the rescue.

I saw her appear to me as I wandered on Earth, inviting me into a higher life, trying to rescue me from what she knew would become of my futile search for fulfillment with the souls stuck on Earth. I had dismissed her as a Shiner, an absurd label for this radiant being. Coming to me in such a low realm was a sacrifice. She had to dim herself, empty herself of glory to even be comprehensible to my fragmented consciousness on Earth.

I then saw her standing with me in this world, offering her love, her generous embrace to one so closed, so self-protected. But her warmth infected me, opened me, so that I could allow her to teach me my first baby steps in awakening to the life and reality of another.

The scene came to the present moment as she entered the temple and approached me and my guardian. I fell at her feet. It took a great act of will, no doubt helped by my guardian, not to make this moment about my contrition. I was able to recognize my remorse for what it was: not an opportunity for self-pity or groveling, but a pure love for her, for her children, and for her husband.

The boundaries between herself and everything she loved were thin. Her life was only barely contained in the size and shape of human form. Her consciousness extended outward like a flowering tree.

"What are you doing down there?" she said, laughing. "Stand up." She took my hand and raised me to my feet. "We are fellow servants. One not better than the other."

"Can you forgive me?" I said. I had nothing else to say. No explanation, no excuses.

"My friend, can you forgive *me* for holding you in Hell, at least in my heart?"

I could hardly comprehend that she had any need for my forgiveness. But no more words were necessary. Grace and light encircled our hearts.

"Our work together is done for now," she said. "But our friendship is eternal." With this she left, and I stood with my guardian in the darkness, basking in the warmth that still lingered.

It was time to continue with my review. I still could not let go completely. The event was not purified entirely. The scenes related to her children and husband embedded in my body again.

My guardian said, "The time will come when you can make peace with them separately. The fragments created that night affected many souls, so healing will come from many souls. You will not be entirely free until the hearts of her children turn to you.

That night your life was entangled with hers in a profound way. But hers is not the life that most binds your consciousness. We must continue this process for that work to unfold. We must attend to the work of turning your heart to your father."

In the beauty of the moment, I had almost forgotten the purpose of this preparation. Though I could not see them directly, I sensed my ancestors gathering around us, ready to observe this process. This was not a spectacle for their entertainment. Their lives were intertwined with mine, and I sensed great anticipation from them.

They would accompany me into Hell, I realized. They would help me rescue my father. I had hoped that my preparation would be extensive, giving me plenty of time to get ready, but I somehow knew the time of the rescue was drawing near.

20

My guardian held his hand in front of me, drawing out more scenes, proceeding backwards from the wreck. The three-dimensional images exploded from my body in a steady stream, projecting into the space before us. I no longer saw the images in a linear sequence of cause and effect. They were a timeless whole, overlapping one another, connecting to one another in ways I never imagined possible.

A conversation at dinner was improbably interwoven with events from years earlier. Getting angry with someone in traffic when I was thirty-five was tied to arguments I had months earlier with your mother. There was no past, present, and future. Moments existed neither in isolation nor in a logical sequence of cause and effect. They branched organically in all directions.

And I did not experience the events as my individual self. As an observer, I not only had access to my own consciousness, my own ego-driven perspectives, but also to others'. I saw how everything I did, even seemingly small things, affected the environment around me. Invisible waves of spiritual energy broadcasted like a radio beacon from my body and either lightened or darkened the collective energies of whomever surrounded me.

I saw myself at college parties, binge drinking to impress friends and hooking up with girls as lost as myself. Never satiated, my appetites grew with indulgence, always needing bigger fixes. My body was a bottomless pit of need and desire. I attached myself to anyone who could satisfy my needs and dismissed those who could not with indifference.

I met your mother at such a party, two needy souls attaching to one another, hoping to use one another to fill our emptiness, mistaking this need for love. It was into these circumstances you were born. We married after living together for five years after your birth. Then, five years after that, she decided it was time for her to move on, to fulfill dreams cut short by your birth. We separated without bitterness.

In our early years we fought terribly, fights that you witnessed all too often, blaming each other directly or indirectly for not meeting needs. We saw each other as investments that were failing to produce the expected return. But by the time we separated permanently, we had at least matured enough to stop blaming. We understood, if only intuitively, that we were two empty souls and that emptiness cannot fill emptiness.

The scenes of my life played on. Even daily interactions with others opened before me, moments I thought were insignificant. Here, a missed chance to say hello. There, avoiding asking someone how they were doing when I sensed they might actually open up and tell me. Then the thing with the money—how had I forgotten?—when I sold a friend's motorcycle for more than he expected, and kept the difference.

It wasn't all bad, of course. I had moments of kindness, real kindness, not the fake stuff to get something I wanted. When these moments—a smile, a hello, concern for another—appeared before us, my guardian celebrated.

In one such scene I was in an airplane, coming home from a business conference. A woman sitting near me could not quiet the child she carried on her lap. The boy would not stop wailing, and he had a particularly shrill and obnoxious cry. The passengers grew restless and agitated, casting angry glances in the mother's direction.

Usually I would have been one of them, annoyed that this mother and her child dared inconvenience me, but this time I saw into the reality of the mother, saw how embarrassed and distraught she was, and I empathized with her plight. Perhaps it was that she reminded me of a younger version of my mother. I cannot say for sure, but for a brief moment I did not see them as obstacles to my goal of a peaceful flight, but as fellow beings, fellow travelers on this lonely planet who could use a hand to lighten their load.

I pulled a stuffed toy from my bag, a souvenir I had purchased for you, and offered it to the child. Miraculously, it worked. The tension, visible in the energetic fields of everyone within earshot of the child, dissipated. From the near-omniscient perspective of my review, I saw the mother's heartbeat slow and her blood pressure decrease. And I saw, in my own chest, a glow of warmth that was, sadly, not a very common sight in the review of my life. This warmth was not self-congratulation for having been a nice guy, the hero of the moment, but a kind of brotherly love for this stranger whom I would never see again.

My guardian acted as if I had rescued orphans from a burning building. His joy was not patronizing, not a pat on the head to make me feel better about the failures in my life. He saw this act from a higher perspective than I was capable of understanding. It set off a chain reaction of consequences, somehow liberating members of my soul family in a small way from ties that still bound them.

Seeing this scene was both gratifying and heartbreaking. I was happy to know I had done something good. I wasn't proud, but simply felt joy experiencing this event in the full light of consciousness. But understanding that such a small act bore significant fruit, I regretted the many opportunities for kindness I had passed up as I pursued my own agenda.

Even more painful were the times when I had snapped at daily irritations, like snatching a bag of burgers from the drive through attendant because my order had taken longer than expected. In far too many instances I let people know they had failed to serve me according to my expectations.

Many times my guardian had to lovingly encourage me to continue, to fully comprehend the situations so I could release them and offer the experiences to God and my spiritual family, the vastness of which I still had not glimpsed.

So I continued to live, not relive, these moments. In mortality, I passed through life as if in a bad dream. Now I was not dreaming, but viewing the dream in the full light of day. My son, you do not need to know all I saw. Someday you too will have your chance to see with eyes undimmed by the weaknesses of mortality.

Much of what I saw was good. I saw myself holding you as a baby, kissing your soft, squishy cheeks, smelling your sweet, tender skin, laced with a hint of baby powder and freshly washed blankets. But my love always mixed with fear. I imagined you suffocating in the night on a poorly placed blanket, falling from a table you climbed, contracting some rare childhood disease. Sometimes I let go of those fears, maybe just from mental exhaustion, and allowed myself to be present as I held you.

When you slept in my arms, it felt as if I were also sleeping, like your calmness, the presence of your spirit, overcame my usual anxiety. In these moments our role reversed and it felt as if you were protecting me, and in a sense you were, standing like a mighty sentinel between me and the nihilism that always threatened, ready to engulf me in despair.

When I held you, I held hope. I had no God at that time in my life, apart from the gods I had created in my image, but you were a constant affirmation of life, of belief in the future in spite of the cynicism and pessimism that usually dominated my thoughts. In those moments I swore to you it would be different between us, different than it was with my father.

But I unknowingly expected you to carry the load of that difference. Though I did not know and would not have admitted it, I was not expecting myself to be a better father so much as I expected you to be a better son. My own failures, not my father's, disgusted me, and so I saddled you with the burden of becoming a better version of myself. I would not let you make my mistakes and repeat my weaknesses.

As you grew older, those weaknesses came out. And so I watched your every movement, looking for signs of what I hated in myself.

Missed a spot raking the lawn? Someday that will get your lazy butt fired from a job. Scared to jump off that rock at the lake, not more than six feet high? You see that little girl over there, half your age? She's been doing it. She isn't scared. No? Okay then, pack your stuff. We're leaving. I don't want to swim with a little chicken. It's embarrassing. No, don't you dare cry. Get over here and stop making a scene. I'm being mean? The world is mean. Someday you'll thank me for toughening you up, just like my dad toughened me up.

Your bony, shivering body, dripped lake water and tears. Oh, how I wished, as a spirit, I could protect you from myself. In every case, although I would swear I was only interested in your success, my actions were always about my image and my goals.

Your mother also came under my condemnation for doing too much or too little of something regarding you. *A new bike for Easter? Not even a real holiday. You know, I had to earn my bike when I was his age?* She was by turns too permissive, too coddling, too controlling, and then, later, too uninvolved. It is little wonder she moved out just after your tenth birthday, leftover cake still in the fridge. I had so assumed control over your destiny that I caused her motherhood to be an unbearable burden rather than the joy it should have been.

After she moved out, she allowed me to be the custodial parent as she returned to college. Without her balancing spirit in the home, the relationship between you and I soured even more in your teenage years. I seemed almost incapable of finding joy in you as the darkness of my ego blinded my eyes to the holiness, the sacredness of your being, having forgotten the gift you were to my soul.

In one scene I watched you share a triumph at school with me—an unexpected good grade on an exam. You downplayed it when you told me about it, not wanting to appear too earnest, too excited. You tested the waters to see my reaction, and if I had responded positively, you were prepared to gush and tell me every detail. Your heart beat with anticipation, hoping for a favorable response. Your whole body cried out for some sign of approval and affection, but I turned away with indifference, even boredom, for this was not the accomplishment I had envisioned for you.

"Hmm, not bad," I said, but you could feel my indifference, and your heart closed. Your spirit could feel the truth, regardless of what I said with my lips. Unconsciously you resolved to give me what I deserved, to pull away from me whenever I felt like it was time to be the caring father. And so I watched moment after painful moment as we descended into mutual resentment and suspicion. We made ourselves into one another's victim. I was the jerk dad, and you were the lazy, disrespectful son who didn't know how good he had it in comparison with my childhood. We fulfilled one another's expectations perfectly.

As you grew older, our fights grew worse, even violent. By the time you moved out, our spirits were so hardened, so desensitized, that the threat of doing physical harm to one another became a painfully real prospect.

Many times during this process my guardian would stop the review, sometimes at my request, to allow me to fully experience it—not to wallow in it, but to completely release it. He often prayed for me, calling down power from on high, for I saw light entering me, strengthening me.

My guardian seemed to be saving the last fight, the one in which you finally left, until I was better at resisting the urge to turn scenes into stories of my own sorrow and remorse, and could instead examine them for the truth they wished to tell.

21

I knew the fight scene must be coming, and when it finally came from my body, I immediately felt a weight lift. It was now before me in all its detail, all of its emotions, all of its causes and effects laid out in a complex, entangled network.

The trigger for the fight was a test I devised for you, having decided you had grown up too lazy, that the pampering your mother spoiled you with in your younger years had made you weak and entitled. I had to balance her permissiveness now. So one day I gave you a list of chores in the house and the yard. I gave you no deadline. It was as if I was daring you to dismiss me.

It was not the first such test, but in the others I would badger you until you complied. In this case, I waited for you to take responsibility and do the work without constant hounding. With each passing day you failed the test, and I gathered evidence for my case against you, against your mother, and against my own regrettable role in failing to teach you when you were young. If this list of chores had been about love and concern, I could have taught you with love and concern, even firmness. But it was not about that. I was daring you to fail. Part of me wanted you to fail to justify my feelings toward you.

Every time you got in your car to leave, every time you watched TV, and every time you went to bed with the work unfinished, I simmered in anger concealed just beneath a calm surface. It was not a matter of the chores needing to be done. It was not a matter of teaching you work ethic. Your every lapse was a confirmation that I had been too easy on you. Compared to my own father, I was too easy, too willing to overlook. And I heard the echo of my father's voice, though long dead, saying that there was no way he would have put up with that kind of disrespect.

Kids these days get away with murder, my father's voice told me, and all they need is an old-fashioned lesson in respect. The hard way.

But no. I had read the books. I would parent differently. I was trying not to repeat his mistakes, but it was not working. You were not becoming what I needed you to become. I owned and amplified your every weakness, and I saw all of them, every slip up, even when they weren't there. People would tell me what a good kid you were, and my feeling was that they hadn't seen you behind closed doors. Why couldn't I see the truth they saw. Whatever you did was never quite good enough.

And now, to dismiss my request for help was to fail each moment. *Kids these days are lazy, disrespectful, and entitled.* I had a number of stories at my reach to condemn you and to turn this problem into some grand narrative about the downfall of society.

One evening you grabbed your car keys and said you were going out with friends. I told you in false calmness that no, you weren't going anywhere, because you had not finished what I had asked you to do. You said you had forgotten and asked for leniency just this one time. It was then I blew up, unleashing my fury on you. You had not forgotten, you were just lazy, and more than that, you were arrogant enough to think you could talk your way out of anything, just as you always had with your mother. But now you were going to learn something different.

In that moment, I saw only defiance in you, but now, from the objectivity of my review, I could see the real shock in you from my reaction, the pain you felt as you looked into my eyes and saw my disgust. You knew, your spirit knew, that this had nothing to do with chores, but was built-up resentment just waiting for the chance to unleash its awful power. This time you did not cower as you so often had, a behavior I had also interpreted as unmanly and weak. Now you stood up for yourself, puffed out your chest, and got in my face.

I told you to step back, and you didn't. I threw you against the wall. You threw a fist and connected with my throat with surprising strength. For a moment I couldn't breathe, but I caught your next swing and twisted your arm around your back and pressed your face into the wall as your left hand flailed impotently, trying to connect with me. My liquor-laced breath spoke threats into your ear, asking if you really wanted to take me on, if you were certain you were ready to play tough guy.

My son, you know these awful details. We lived it together. But what I didn't know in the first living of it, but now saw in this second living, was how totally and utterly we failed to see one another's reality, the sacredness of our being. Each of us saw the other only as an object of failure, failure to perform as expected in some way. In every way, perhaps.

A spark of awareness came as I held you against the wall. I had not touched you in many years, not even for a hug, reasoning that my own father never stood for that sort of affection. But now as I held your body I felt its anger, its life, the hardness of your muscles, your sweaty skin pressed against mine, struggling against me, fighting for freedom. For the first time since I held you as a child, I felt your aliveness. You were strong now. You had will and determination. And I was holding you down, holding you too tight, for you cried out in pain. I released you, hoping now that you would leave and be safe from me.

I asked my guardian to stop the review. I had had enough. I was prepared to stop whatever opportunities for growth this universe held. I was not worthy to move on. As I turned my attention to him, I noticed that as the scenes turned to my relationship with you, my son, he was experiencing pain as deep as mine. Even though his face was veiled, his agony was unmistakable. Angelic beings whom I somehow knew were my ancestors appeared in the darkness of the temple to strengthen not only me but him, pouring light into his soul as well. Love and compassion and, above all, a deep gratitude emanated from them.

But seeing that my life was as difficult for my guardian to watch as it was for me, I refused to continue. It was one thing for me to see my mistakes, but to bring this beautiful being low with my bad choices was a crime. I would not continue.

"You don't understand," he said. "You heal with these lashes; countless lives are healed."

The scene still sat before us as if waiting for my cue, waiting to know whether it would re-enter my body as an object of light and wisdom or as darkness and pain. The question depended on where I went next, whether I picked up the threads and continued the work of unraveling. I saw that these threads led to scenes from my childhood with my father. But I did not want to go there. I was willing to rescue my father from Hell, but not to relive my life with him.

"I thought I was on a rescue mission," I objected. "What does all this have to do with our mission?"

"We are here now," he said. "This is the entry point into your father's Hell. He needs you now. The rescue begins here."

22

The threads of light and energy looped around us in a beautiful dance of color. I could see that they led to darker scenes, perhaps leading all the way down to Hell. Maybe my connection with my father would be the pathway, the trail that would lead us to him in that abyss. Horrible memories of that sad and dreary existence flooded my mind. Reluctantly, I allowed my consciousness to move through the pathways connected to my fight with you. But the scenes that burst into the hologram were not of Hell, but of a similar fight I had with my father.

I was shocked to see the ways in which I had carried my own father's attitudes and inclinations. I spent so much of my life running from him, trying to define myself as different from him, and I had believed that I was successful. But the scene that lay before me was almost indistinguishable from the one that played out moments before. The threads here were tightly interwoven. It would have been impossible to cleanse one event without cleansing the other.

Our fight was similar but even more violent, with

me ending up with a broken lip and bruised cheek, marks for which I had to make unlikely excuses the next day at school. And like my fight with you, mine with my father led to me moving out.

At this point in the review, things took an unexpected turn. Suddenly all scenes were related to my relationship with my father, and each of those scenes was connected to his life. We were seeing his life now, but I experienced it as my own, or at least the distinction between us melted away. I saw my father's birth right after World War II. His father, my grandpa, fought in the Pacific. Though they didn't have a name for it then, his father suffered from post-traumatic stress disorder. He would wake in the middle of the night to pace the house, checking multiple times on my own father as he slept peacefully in a crib.

Only after drinking enough gin to numb the fear could he drift off to sleep on the couch. From this point of view I could both feel and see the fear, how it spilled from his body and saturated the walls and floors and furniture of the house. It affected everyone, especially his wife and my infant father.

I saw my father grow up in that home, a home of constant low-level anxiety, even paranoia. My grandmother walked on eggshells, never certain what comment, what image, what sound might trigger either screaming rage or trembling fear. Nearly every night he paced the hallways, checking on his sleeping children, peering suspiciously through windows, testing locked doors. Sometimes he carried his side arm, a .45 caliber pistol, in his belt as he paced and drank, and would often fall asleep with it on his chest, rising and falling with each breath.

My grandfather's fear found an outlet in hatred, and he compiled a long list of things he hated—the government, the Japanese, and eventually his own wife and children when they failed to hate with his same intensity. My father was constantly harassed for the ease of his life compared to how terrible it had been during the depression and then the war. This generation, spoiled with their muscle cars and drive-in cafes, had no idea what real sacrifice was. They didn't know patriotism. They didn't know work. They didn't know loyalty to God and family.

My father bore the weight of this abuse with surprising meekness. He did not lash out. He saw his father's disturbed mind clearly and even felt compassion for him, taking steps to protect him from himself, or, to avoid family shame, keep his drunken eccentricities from public view.

I was surprised to see my father was a gentle and caring soul from his childhood. He had a difficult time trapping mice or, at his mother's insistence, smashing spiders in the house. On one occasion, he spent several weeks and countless hours nurturing a small kitten he struck with his truck. When it finally died of an infection, he buried it in a corner of the yard under the cloak of darkness, so his father wouldn't see his tears.

He was especially gentle with his mother and two sisters. The despairing and hardened man I had known bore little resemblance to the boy I saw growing up. One night, after his father threw an empty gin bottle through the window, believing it to be a grenade, and stormed out of the house into some imaginary battle, he picked up the shards and patched the window with electrical tape and cardboard. He then made his mother a cup of tea and held her as she wept.

He read bedtime stories to his sisters to drown out the sound of his parents arguing downstairs. He was a peacemaker, always trying to bring calm to the household, usually through pleading prayers. From a young age, his was the task of patching a leaky dam that always threatened to burst and sweep his family away in a flood of madness and violence.

I watched one scene in which he had worked and saved for a Sony radio, a new product in the 1950s that American teens were snatching up by the thousands. He had kept the savings and the purchase a secret. But one day his father discovered it while patrolling the home.

The radio symbolized all that my grandfather hated: spoiled children, the Japanese who had not sufficiently paid for their war crimes, and the emergence of Rock 'n Roll. For weeks he punished my father for this betrayal and, in his more delusional and drunken states, claimed the "Jap radio" was a spy instrument that transmitted their location to Japanese intelligence. He blamed my father for compromising their position to the enemy and smashed it against the wall.

The day after he graduated from high school, my father left this troubled home, feeling great relief mixed with guilt. He felt as though he were abandoning his mother and sisters but knew of no other way to maintain his own sanity. He worked odd jobs for a few years, sneaking extra money to his mother, before being drafted into the Vietnam War. Going to war was the only thing he did that made his father proud.

The scene shifted to the war, and we were on a drizzly jungle hillside. Scenes from the war played out in horrific detail. I saw, to my amazement, that he was a terrible soldier. When I was a child, the few stories I had been told of his war years were of valor and endurance. But what I saw before me now was a frightened teenager clutching a cold, wet M16, praying for the strength to make it through another day.

In firefights, he spent his time hiding for the most part, never advancing the fight, firing his weapon as a token to appear he was at least doing something. He was usually placed in stations of secondary importance, as he could not be relied on to hold a position. I saw into his thoughts as he fantasized daily of deserting the army and dreamt, unrealistically, of wandering into a remote section of jungle and living out the war peacefully in a grass hut, eating whatever he could find.

I hurt for him as I watched these scenes play out. I had a hard time believing this was my father. It seemed I was watching the life of another man, a man I had never met, a man too kind and compassionate for his own good, way out of his depth for such a tender soul. His greatest fear was not of getting killed, but of killing. For this was a young man, as I had witnessed in an earlier scene, who refused, to the disappointment and mockery of his father, to kill a rooster brought home from a friend's farm. When his father finally killed the bird, he refused to eat the meat that night, not out of protest, but from the shame of lacking the courage to provide Sunday dinner.

Much of the war passed without him having to kill anyone, at least no one that he could see directly, as most of the fighting consisted of shots fired into thick undergrowth or aimed at distant targets.

It wasn't until he was halfway through the war that he experienced his first kill. He was ambushed on patrol in the early morning hours, still dark enough that the fiery flashes from machine guns shone brightly against the dull gray of the jungle. He was able to find cover by jumping into a shallow trench, realizing too late the trench was occupied by a frightened twelve-year-old Vietcong fumbling desperately, raising his AK-47. My father, also fumbling, raised his gun first and fired a burst of three rounds into the boy.

My father watched as the child took his last breaths, pawing at the mud until finally becoming still. The shock of this moment entered my father's body with devastating force. His whole mind and body were numb. Every cell trembled with remorse and pain. The weight of it crushed him. He couldn't breathe. The sounds of fighting faded away as he struggled for his breath. When he regained awareness, the fighting was over. It was a minor ambush, comprising mostly of young teens from a nearby village. They had been eliminated.

For the rest of the war, he was not the same person. He grew into something more familiar to me, a man choked by persistent despair and cynicism. Caring had been too painful, so he stopped caring about anything. He stopped feeling. Before the war, and until his first kill, he had declined many opportunities to drink and smoke pot. He had seen what these things had done to his father and wanted to keep them out of his life. But now they were necessary to keep from caring and feeling.

Sitting in the trenches and dugouts, a new disease took hold of him, an idea that, once thought, could not be unthought. His fantasies about leaving the war now turned to fantasies about leaving this life. Living in a grass hut in the jungle was not realistic, but putting his rifle in his mouth or lying on a grenade—those could be done. He would not have been the first. It would be cowardly, he knew, but it provided two possibilities, both of which had their appeal. Either there was no life after death, and he would escape into oblivion where there was no such thing as cowardice or bravery, or he would go to Hell where he could pay for the crime of killing a child. This latter option was his preference. Fantasizing about the purifying punishment he would receive in such a place became a new pastime.

He never pulled the trigger. His tour of duty came to an end, and he left the war. But like so many others, the war never left him. He was unrecognizable to his mother and sisters. When he drank beer with his father, they never mentioned the war. They only drank in mutual silence, in mutual understanding that nothing needed to be said.

The scenes of his life continued to unfold, and I was able to comprehend vast amounts of information with only a glance at the images. That he was able, years after the war, to pull himself together enough to find my mother, was a miracle, an act of grace. They met at a time when he was making great efforts to rebuild his life and had entered into a seminary to become a pastor. His own family had never been particularly religious, but from a young age he had a sort of religious instinct, a natural affinity for stories of Jesus and for prayer. Though this instinct received little nurturing, it never entirely left him until the war, when he felt betrayed by God.

Entering the seminary was his attempt to reclaim God or find answers to the problem of suffering. But the theological treatise, the theories upon theories about God, the competing models, the divisive schools of thought, left him empty. He thirsted for God but found in his courses only antique bottles, empty and covered with dust. He dropped out of school angry about God and religion, but also sought them more desperately after leaving the seminary.

From this point he spiraled downward toward an end I remembered too well. Maybe that's what made this so hard to watch. I knew where these scenes would lead.

23

My mother, who thought she had married a future preacher, now tried to come to terms with being married to both Saul and Paul all in the same person. I perceived this contradiction as hypocrisy, for while he insisted that I go to church with my mother, he would disappear for the entire afternoon every Sunday. I had assumed that he was off fishing or drinking or both, but now saw that he would go on long, tormented walks, one moment supplicating God and another yelling at Him.

The alcohol and drugs that numbed him in Vietnam now served the same purpose, but were more abundant, more available. Going to church every Sunday under these conditions became such a ridiculous sham that at age fourteen I refused to go anymore, declaring myself agnostic, a term I had only recently learned and latched on to as my new identity.

I saw now how my abandonment of faith affected

my father, for he saw in it his own failure. He had imagined that, while his own soul was lost, he would at least produce a good and believing son as a kind of atonement for his sins. My own rejection of God showed him all that he hated about himself. Our fights became increasingly violent as he tried to beat out of me every attribute he despised in himself.

When I left home as a junior in high school and moved into a friend's house to finish my last year, his decline was severe. No longer violent, no longer angry, he withdrew into himself, surrounding himself with an impenetrable solitude. The only objects of his affection were his horse and dog. I was jealous of the attention he gave them. Unlike me, in whom he had invested all his hopes for redemption, he expected nothing from his animals, and was therefore free to love them.

I knew none of this during my life, but now I could see the quiet moments he spent with his animals, the way he caressed them and cared for them. I saw that under different circumstances, my father might have been a Saint Francis. His reverence for life, even during these disturbed years, remained.

The portrait of my father's life came into clear view, and it bore little resemblance to the memories I had formed in mortality, memories that made me the victim of nearly every interaction. The man I saw now was a hero, given the challenges he faced. I saw into his soul with clarity and found a gentle and loving spirit.

Another scene unfolded. Days after one of our fights, I came home to find a puppy, a small yellow lab, sitting in my room. I was mortified. I wondered if it was a gift and hoped that it wasn't. I did not know how to receive it. And I could see now that it was indeed a gift, and my father did not know how to give it. I saw that he had pondered ways to find something in common with me for several days, something we could share. He bought the dog after much thought, and at a high price, but could not allow himself to give it as a gift openly. It would make him appear weak and vulnerable, and he knew his father would disapprove of catering to a child in such a way.

When I brought the puppy out in my arms, he held back a smile and hardened himself slightly.

"I thought it could teach you some responsibility," he said.

I could see now in the review that this was not his intent at all. Now, able to see into his spirit, I saw that he had daydreamed of the two of us taking our dogs to the lake. He had daydreamed of teaching me how to train the pup. He had imagined, in great detail, that we would laugh together, that I would come to him with questions about the dog and that he would give wise answers.

But all he could think to say, in the moment, to hide his tenderness, was that the animal would teach me some responsibility. I poured the puppy some food and water, then left it, returning to my room in silence. My intentional neglect of the dog over the next several months was the cause, at least on the surface, of the fighting that led me to move in with my friend across town.

Shortly after I left home, he accidentally backed over the puppy. Watching this in the review, I lunged forward to save the dog, screamed for him to stop, but there was no use. I was seeing recorded images, events that had already happened.

I was not trying to save the puppy; I was trying to save him, for I knew this was the event that began his descent into darkness. The dog was his last effort to connect with me; now he had killed it and killed me also, or so he imagined it, seeing my room empty and packed up.

He spiraled into a depression from which he would not recover. He was no longer angry, no longer disappointed; he simply surrounded himself with a veil of silence. My mother gave me reports of his decline, how worried she was, how living with him had grown dark. I told her that I would move back in, but she refused, saying she did not know if I would be safe. At least he was quiet now, and if I moved back there was no telling what old problems it would trigger.

Maybe to ease my conscience, my immature teenage self imagined that his condition was a consequence of his own choices. I told myself that only he could work out his problems and that his issues had nothing to do with me.

But now, as I watched the review, no such thoughts were present. I felt only compassion for this gentle soul who, in other circumstances, would have been a happy and loving person. So when I watched him load his old dog into his truck one rainy November day while carrying a military issue .45 caliber pistol—a weapon he had not fired in 20 years— my heart broke.

At the lake he scribbled a note that was simply an

apology to me, my mother, and his sisters. For nearly an hour he tenderly stroked his old dog, and then he poured it large bowls of food and water. He told the dog to stay, and it obeyed. Then he wandered into the bushes. Even then he was worried about what his dog might see, taking care to be just out of sight so as not to confuse or disturb it.

Even so, the dog whimpered at the sound of the single gunshot that rang out from the leafless trees.

I cried out for him to stop but knew I was seeing events that were already history. There was nothing I could do about it now, but I was reminded why I was here, why I was witnessing these things, and that there was still something I could do to help.

24

I watched my father emerge from the bushes fully alive and bewildered. For a moment I hoped against all reason that he had survived somehow, that perhaps I was seeing some alternate reality with a happier ending than the one I lived with for all those years. But then he returned to the undergrowth to look at his body lying in the weeds. He inspected the fatal wound, horrified at what he had done but confused at observing his own body in this way. What was that sad, pale flesh? The landscape grew dim and shadowy, almost as if a mist had risen from the Earth to block the sunlight.

He was still him. Still with his thoughts, his memories, his regrets. The fantasies he entertained of either slipping into oblivion or being sent to a fiery Hell by a just God did not happen.

A third option presented itself now, the one he had refused to consider. A column of warm and loving light appeared several feet above the darkening landscape. It opened into a tunnel that shimmered and sparkled with life. It drew energy into itself, as if it were trying to gather my father's spirit into its warmth and safety. He approached the light, answering its invitation, drawn by a sense of belonging.

But from the shadows behind him came another voice. It was not just one voice but the voice of legions. "That is no place for you," they said. "You know that you're a killer. You know you don't deserve it."

He hesitated and his face sunk as if gravity pulled with greater force. In the light he had forgotten himself; he had forgotten his story for a brief instant. But now he was easily persuaded. Killer of men. Unworthy. Unholy.

He turned from the light to the shadows where his body lay. The voices became stronger, more insistent.

"We will help you hide. We have a dark and quiet place where you won't hurt anyone. It's just this way through the trees." I recognized the hideous sound of hushed laughter. I recognized the sound of barely concealed cruelty waiting for the right moment to attack.

The light seemed to intensify, and the love coming from it was offered without condition. It was not a prize to be claimed, but an invitation to return home. When my father glanced its way again, the voices from the shadows cried out.

"The light knows what you've done, and now it's time to pay the price. You belong with us."

His shoulders carried the weight of every wrong he had ever committed, and carrying this burden had engrained itself into his very identity. He guarded his pain jealously. The pain was his alone, and he would not share it with anyone, especially not God. He walked toward the shadows.

The invitation to hide drew him in, not as a way to escape pain, but as a way to hide from a love he could not comprehend. He walked deeper into the shadows, hungry to receive retribution for his deeds, a desire that his welcoming committee, having long helped cultivate his pain and despair, was happy to fulfill. He disappeared from my view into that demented world and I cried out, knowing where he was going, knowing what awaited him. I knew how easy it would be for deranged souls to manipulate his once-receptive mind, how open he would be to their dark lies.

I cried out for him to stop. My body shuddered as I lost sight of him and heard the beginnings of a hideous frenzy.

I withdrew from the scene, and now the record of his whole life floated before me in perfect three-dimensional reality. I could see it from beginning to end. Strings of light coiling and branching, connecting and branching out again. Each tendril of energy was imbedded with images, intelligence, and wisdom. His life was worth saving. *He* was worth saving. Where he saw only failure, I now saw only beauty. I saw a loving and tender child whose goodness was never given the conditions to flourish. I saw his mistakes and pain, but these were also beautiful as they formed a tapestry of rich human experience. I saw the many misunderstandings between us and how he always did the best he could with the emotional and mental resources he had.

I saw the many moments when, after he had snapped at me, brought me to tears with some scolding, he would come into my bedroom at night, not wanting to be seen because his own training had taught him that men do not cry over their children. He would apologize to me, even touch my cheek or stroke my hair sometimes, leaving abruptly when I stirred, fearing I would catch him loving me in a way he could never allow himself when I was awake.

But now I *was* awake. God had awakened me from my own nightmares. I craved my father's love in the full light of day—no shame, no hiding.

I had assumed during this process that I was being shown his life so that I could forgive him enough to want to rescue him, but now it was I who needed rescue. It was I who needed forgiveness from this magnificent spirit that I had so misjudged and misunderstood.

My guardian stood near me. Joy and gratitude poured from his presence. He did not have to urge me to the rescue mission now. No angel of Heaven or demon of Hell could have kept me from plunging into the depths of that dark region.

My father would indeed be struck down by lightning, the lightning of my love and of God's love. He did not deserve to be where he was, and I would never rest until he knew it.

"I am ready now," I told my guardian. I had never been so convicted, so passionate about anything in my life.

"Are you certain?" he asked. "Are you sure you

really want to see him as he is?"

"Yes," I replied. "I am ready now. It must be now."

Energy swirled and gathered around me in ribbons of light, then opened into a vortex above me. I waited for a portal to open a gate to Hell, into which our rescue mission would plunge. But the vortex was not a portal to Hell; it was a cleansing whirlwind that gathered the thousands of scenes before me—my entire life and parts of my father's life.

The once dark and heavy images began to crackle with light and energy. They were not being erased, but transformed. The images themselves remained unchanged, but now they shimmered with love and wisdom. They were still part of me, but had become part of everything else as well. They were now absorbed into the universal body of Christ, purified and sanctified.

I sensed that thousands of ancestors gathered to witness and celebrate. Whatever we were doing was affecting them in profound ways I did not comprehend.

My guardian looked at me with warmth and love. With him at my side, I knew we could go into Hell and overcome it together.

He asked me again, "Are you certain that you would go back into Hell to rescue someone as undeserving as that old man?"

"Yes," I said again. "It has to happen now. He has to know. He has to know that I love him, that I'm sorry."

With these words it seemed the very person of my guardian would be consumed in fiery light. His love washed over me in waves.

"My son," he said, "your love has already rescued me."

My heart knew the meaning of these words even before the veil lifted from my eyes, revealing the person of my earthly father, my friend, my guardian.

We embraced as father and son, finally seeing the truth in one another, knowing one another for the first time. Our mutual forgiveness and love sent waves of purifying energy through the fabric of our ancestral family, cleansing and empowering unseen millions of souls. Our spirit bodies, feeling almost as if they would merge into one, rose into a higher dimension.

"How is this possible?" I said.

"They got me too. Seeing you in Hell was all it took. I had helped those lost souls hunt you, but letting us see each other was a mistake. I could see you. Through the scales of darkness that covered both of us, I could still see you. Soon after that, God sent guardians to cut away my chains and make me a hunter of souls."

When I apprenticed myself to the master hunter in Hell, my father was in the care of the true Master, learning the art of rescue. I should have known that God, in his mercy, would not allow such a precious soul to linger in Hell very long. If he could rescue one such as I, of course he was capable of rescuing my father.

When we left the temple, we were in a different realm now. A group of beautiful souls gathered to greet us. I knew them intimately somehow, though not from my mortal life. They were ancient friends whose lives were mine just as mine was theirs. When I embraced them their life poured into me, and my consciousness grew, as if I were no longer just one person, but two, three, many.

This one, a farmer from old England, who, as we embraced, gave me the gift of his life, the morning chores, the dew on the grass, how he confided in his milk cow like an old friend. A woman from France, 18th century, pulled me in. She loved music and played the piano. I heard it echo in the spacious halls of her home in Paris. Then financial ruin, a move to a small cottage, her sadness as she tapped her fingers against a stained kitchen table, hearing the notes only in her memory. All of it was beautiful now. Beauty from ashes. No regret, no injustice. I understood each one I embraced, and they understood me. And this understanding was love, for to understand, to truly comprehend another, is to love them.

*

And it is here I dwell now, my son, as I continue to make reconciliation and learn the mysteries of God's creations.

This new kingdom is not the end of my journey to God, but it is here I am beginning to taste what it means to find rest in the Lord. I do not need to be somebody important. I do not need to impress or cultivate an image or pass a test or even "progress" in the earthly sense of gaining prestige and influence. I am not greater than or less than anything or anyone else in creation. The self, that old burden from mortality, is dying, and with it, all its concerns.

And what rises in its place is the freedom to love and be loved. It's inexhaustible. It never grows old. On Earth, my life was a relentless quest to find new stimulation, but everything I found disappointed in the end. It grew stale and boring. But the love I live and breathe here is not a sensation or emotion one can get used to. It is not an experience that becomes normal over time. It is ever new, ever present. And yet I am told it is still not the fullness we journey toward.

My father teaches me and is also taught. The man at my side is not the same man I thought I knew on Earth. One is real, and the other is fiction. I never knew him on Earth. All I knew was a story I had created about him, and I thought that story was him. And I made you into a story as well, as you did me. But none of the stories were true.

The story I have just told you is not me. But the mortal mind works in stories and they serve a purpose in their own way. Someday the veil of ignorance will be lifted from our eyes and we will see one another as we truly are.

With each new awakening I grow in wisdom and grace, yet as the heavens continuously open to me I become more a child in my understanding. I wish I could convey the wonders that await. But even more I wish I could help you see the grace that surrounds you in your present world, in this very moment. We cannot comprehend the grace of higher worlds until we see the grace of the present reality in which we find ourselves.

In life I did not teach you this by precept or by example. This failure still hurts and will until you and I can embrace in love and forgiveness. I think of the lost opportunities for love that I squandered in my own self-absorbed life. It hurts to think of what might have been, how easy it would have been to reach out to you, to speak a word of kindness, or to offer fatherly love and wisdom. I wish I could reach out and touch you now as I speak this tale into your soul. But dimensions of time and space separate us. I am only a whisper in the dark.

Yet I am part of the work, God's great work and glory of binding hearts and minds of the human family until none shall be lost. I pray that your heart might begin to soften toward me. My beloved guardian and father stands now at my side with his hand on my shoulder, giving me the strength to love you as God loves, without the need and fear that could draw me back into spaces where I no longer belong.

You have been given the chance to begin anew. The precious life that grows in the womb of the woman who sleeps beside you will change you. I know you have not yet embraced your impending fatherhood and committed yourself fully to the mother of your child. You worry, you fear, and you want to run. I know this because I gave you so many of these fears. We share that burden, so now you are my work, and I will use whatever small influence I have and pray that you won't repeat my mistakes. The greatest way to honor God and your soul family, who work and cheer for your success, is to overcome what they passed on to you.

God in his wisdom has given you a child, a little girl, who will bless those who have passed on and those yet unborn. She will heal broken fragments in our family and create a new thread of light that will reach into the future. I am not yet allowed to see the work God has designed for her. There is much anticipation among our family on this side of the veil as her spirit prepares for the work.

Yet I have been given a glimpse of you in the near future, at least one possibility I pray will unfold. I see your wedding. I see you waking in the middle of the night because your wife is in labor. I see you driving the empty streets, your heart racing as you speak comforting words. The labor comes on fast and you speed through the night. At the hospital you stay by her side and tuck her hair behind her ear and squeeze her hand hard when she asks. You feel the fear that comes when standing at the threshold of life and death. You watch her heart and your baby's heart on the screen and feel each pulse as they beat in rhythm with the heart in your chest. You will hear the first cries and then you will breathe what feels like your first breath all night, your first breath as a father.

I see you welcome this little girl into her mortal life, the beginning of her earthly journey. I see you, feel you, holding her and looking into the depth of her eyes, as you discover love that strikes you like a bolt of lightning, and Grace with power to find you in darkness and draw you patiently, relentlessly, into the Light.

As an author, I enjoy hearing from readers, and I'd love to know your thoughts or questions about *Heaven Will Find You*. I personally read and respond to every email. I also have a special offer for those wishing to order multiple copies for gifts or book clubs.

Please email me at sheldonjohnlawrence@gmail.com or visit www.sheldonlawrence.com

Made in the USA
Las Vegas, NV
04 May 2024

89542005R00121